STAR SEASON

A SCIFI ALIEN ROMANCE

Jove Chambers

Punk Rawk Books

STAR SEASON

www.vjchambers.com

Punk Rawk Books

All characters appearing in this work are fictitious. Any resemblance to real persons, living or dead, is purely coincidental.

ISBN: 9798356842672
PRINTED IN THE UNITED STATES OF AMERICA

10 9 8 7 6 5 4 3 2 1

STAR SEASON

A SCIFI ALIEN ROMANCE

Jove Chambers

ONE

cypra

"It's Star Season, shei," said the man in front of me. He spoke Common with a drawl that seemed to be indicative of the local accent on this planet. The planet itself wasn't populated enough for there to be more than one accent. Ohkk was a planet in the Ohker System, just below the asteroid belt, and it was far too close to its sun to seemingly support life, except for the fact that a large swath of it was covered in a heavy atmosphere that blocked out the sun, keeping temperatures cool enough for life to survive. It was still extremely hot, though, in my opinion. Extremely.

"Yes, I've heard this," I said to him. "From every other guide I've spoken to, all of whom told me they wouldn't be caught dead going up there. When I asked them if there was anyone who would, your name kept coming up."

He chuckled. "Did it?" He was one of two native sentient species on this planet. He was a donen. The other species were greeicx. Both of them were species that vaguely resembled my own species—which was human. However, this didn't mean much. Almost all sentient life in the galaxy seemed to resemble each other. No one knew whether this meant we had a common ancestor or whether life just took a predictable pattern.

He had antlers, tall horns rising up out of his forehead, just in front of his ears, and he was furry. Furry all over, but mostly furry on the bottom from his hips down to the bottom of his legs, which were hooved, not like the feet and digits I had.

He was also naked. They were all naked. They were just furry between their legs, these aliens, and I guessed they were the sort of species whose genitalia had to be coaxed out, which meant I didn't have to stare at their cocks, so I guessed they technically didn't *need* clothes, but it was still a little disconcerting. Their chests were all bare, and only as furry as a human man's might be, so there was a *lot* of bare skin.

Ohkk was a technologically developed planet, not classified as primitive, but there was a good bit of undeveloped land out here, the people who lived on the planet spread out, reliant on a primarily agrarian society to sustain them. If there was a backwoods planet to the galaxy, it was Ohkk.

"But you're saying no, too?" I said.

"Shei," he said. This was not my name. Near as I could gather, it was some local form of endearment for women, something like sweetheart, which I didn't much care for, but I was trying to get this guy to help me, so it didn't make sense to antagonize him. "I'd have to be stupid to go up there during Star Season."

"Or brave," I said. "Which is what the others said about you. 'Only person brave enough to go up to the pole during Star Season I can think of is Halston Effers.'"

He raised his eyebrows under his antlers. "That what they said?" He was amused by me, and I didn't like it.

"Yes," I said. Actually, what they'd said was that he

was the only person *stupid* enough to go up there, but… like I said… not trying to antagonize him.

"Huh," he said, noncommittally. He leaned back in his chair. We were sitting in an open-air bar at a table for two. Everything out here was open air because it was so hot all the time. There was a thatched roof overhead giving shade and fans overhead chugging away, making the air less sweltering. He had a tall glass of whatever the local ale was in these parts. He took a drink of it.

"But you're saying no?" I said again, lifting my chin. "You can't handle it, after all?"

He laughed softly. "What do you want to go up there for, anyway?"

"It's, um, important," I said. "There's a ship that went down. No communication from it, even though we can trace it. We think… they could have survived."

"This is a rescue mission, shei?" He eyed me, the humor going out of his eyes. Now, he looked shrewd, as if he was trying to figure me out, as if he could read truth in my expression.

I wanted to break eye contact. I didn't. "It's… there are things on the ship that we need."

"Who's we?"

"The people I work with," I said.

"Which is?"

"We're a shipping company," I said, lying through my teeth. "Atabong Shipping Ltd. We move all sorts of things back and forth across the galaxy." I did have a manifest and some official-looking paperwork that I could pull out if I needed to verify my story. It should past muster, even with the Toth, who were basically the evil alien overlords who subjugated the galaxy.

You know, the government.

Out here, though, this was kind of the wild. The Toth presence wasn't pronounced, and they shouldn't be poking into anything.

"Shipping company." He nodded. He didn't believe me.

Shit. I squared my shoulders and glared at him. I wondered what he thought of me. Whatever he was thinking, it probably wasn't that I worked for the resistance, and that there were very important tactical schematics for a dangerous weapon on that ship, and that I had to get it if we were going to have a chance at making a stand against the Toth.

"Because if it were a rescue mission, I'm thinking you would have led with that," he said. "So, this is a business problem. That's the 'emergency.' You got some rich client who's angry about his cargo stuck out on a nowhere planet, and now your company is making you risk your life and asking you to hire someone to risk his life just for something on the ship?"

Oh, okay, he *did* believe me. "It's, um…"

"If you got a rich client, though, why aren't you offering more credits for this little walkabout you want to do, straight through the vvoln-infested forests? Why didn't he set you down right on that wreckage, let you go straight down and look for survivors and get his cargo? Too much of a cheapskate to spring for that kind of a mission?"

"We can't get there by ship," I said. "The magnetic nature of the pole is interfering with sensors. It's probably why that ship went down in the first place."

Ohkk wasn't a big planet, so the equator and the poles weren't too far away from each other. With a good speeder, it was a four-hihor journey. The atmosphere that covered the inhabitable part of the planet didn't cover the pole. But because of the pole's tilt, there was a period of time when there was no visible sun there, for the span of about two gemoons. Star Season. You could see the stars up there, and it was starry darkness all the time.

"Right," he said. "Yeah, I guess I can see that." He took a thoughtful drink of his ale. "Even so, I can't do it."

"But why not?" I said. "It's what you do." This guy was a real outdoorsy type. He made his living hunting and selling the meat and pelts of the things he caught and killed. He was supposedly the best of the best and willing to try anything, do anything. I'd heard he'd wrestled one of those vvolns with his bare hands, strangled it to death.

"It's Star Season, shei," he said, shaking his head, and now his voice was a little gentler.

"So what?" I said. "Why does that matter?" I'd asked of the other guys, too, and gotten nothing but embarrassed looks, blushes, snickers of laughter like they were twelve-gecycle-olds.

"Oh, you don't know." He let out another chuckle. "You didn't look it up when you heard the term?"

"I did," I said. "It told me about the tilt of the planet, the atmosphere, but so what? So, it's dark. You can't get me there in the dark?"

"That's all you found out? You didn't read about the history?"

"What, that your people once journeyed up there once a cycle during this time for rituals, but that you stopped because of the dangers of the predators? But you hunt those predators. You can *kill* them."

He rubbed his chin, chuckling again. His chin was furry, like the rest of him, and I found myself noticing that he was attractive. I had tried not to notice this about these odd antlered, naked natives on this planet, but they did have that whole primitive wild man thing going for them, didn't they? I crossed my legs.

He sucked in a breath through his nose and his eyes widened. He let out another laugh, this one a sort of snort.

"What?" I said. "*Can't* you kill them?"

"I, uh, I'd be distracted," he said, and now he was smiling at me, smiling in a way I really didn't like.

"Distracted by what?"

"We didn't go up there in ancient times for a ritual. It was our mating season. There are specific plants that grow in that part of the planet and their pollen triggers a change in our bodies," he said. "We'd all go up there, and it was called a rut. Thin the herd, basically, because you'd either get killed fighting some other guy for a woman to mate, or if you got her, you and she would get taken down by a vvoln while you were, you know, at it."

It was my turn to blush. I looked away, down at the table.

"Your *scent,* shei, I gotta say. I might have to take back everything I say to men who jack off to all that Toth-human porn. You're something else, aren't you?"

My gaze jerked up to his.

He shrugged at me. "Oh, right, your species is like the Toth where you pretend you *can't* smell things, right? Not polite to comment on the fact your pussy's wet and I can tell?"

"Definitely not polite," I said through clenched teeth. "And it's not. Wet, that is. And I don't need your services anyway, so never mind." I got up as quickly as I could, but my legs got tangled up in the chair legs and

I barely managed to extricate myself without knocking it over, but then I lost my balance.

He was next to me—I hadn't even seen him move, he was that fast—gripping my elbow and holding me upright. "Careful there, shei." His voice was deep and almost velvet, and I felt it go all through me, like it went directly to my clit, which twitched.

He let go of me. Holding up both hands in a hands-off gesture. "Sorry."

I shook my head. "No, no, it's me. There's no reason to be…" I tangled a hand in my hair, sighing. "It's inappropriate, this reaction I'm having. I guess, considering the cultural differences, I don't have any right to be that outraged, but—"

"Nah, cultural differences?" He snorted. "That's not the culture around here, not at all. It's me. That was out of line." He furrowed his brow, looking perplexed. "That's not even *like* me."

I squared my shoulders. "It's fine. Let's get back to talking about going up to the pole?"

"Here you are, pretty little human girl on a strange planet, and here I am, other species perving on you. Not my finest hihor. I'd blame it on the season, but if we don't go up there, there's no plant reaction, and we don't get out of control. As a human, I bet you get it a lot."

Humans had been brought to this galaxy to be bred by the Toth after their women died, owing to the similarities between our species. Human girls equaled sex in a lot of people's minds.

I shook my head. "No, not… no." In all honesty, the last time I'd really considered myself as a sexual being had been gecycles ago. All I did was work. I'd thrown myself into my work with the resistance. It wasn't as if there weren't men doing resistance work as well, but I didn't want distractions, and I wasn't the type who handled meaningless hookups well. I tended to get attached and distracted even if I tried not to. Best to just avoid the whole thing.

Honestly, it had been a while since I'd even masturbated. I felt like I'd just turned it all off, that side of myself, and then… here… on a planet with naked men with furry thighs and antlers sticking out of their heads and… what the stars was even going *on* with me?

"Well, then I'm doubly sorry," said Halston Effers. "Look, you better hope whoever was on that ship died when it went down. The vvoln hunt in packs and they like to play with their food. They'll rip things apart but in such a way that you bleed out watching them eat your legs, you know. It's a shitty way to die. But they *are* dead, one way or the other. And if we went up there… well… we can't."

"Because you'd…" I looked down at his crotch. Then away.

"Maybe nothing," he said. "We take suppressants these days. If donen want to mate, it's easier done without going into a frothing-at-the-mouth madness that makes you mount anything in sight and fuck them senseless, right? No one really wants to do that, because you're out of control. It's terrifying. If we want to mate, we take things that allow us to do it without, uh, the rut. And the suppressants are supposed to withstand the pollen in the air from the seasonal changes, even if I went up there."

"Really?" I said. "So, then why won't you?"

He shifted on his hooves. "That's a risk you want to take, shei?"

My clit throbbed again. What the stars was wrong with me? "I need to get there. It's important. We can take a speeder, right? How bad could it really be? We couldn't be there for longer than a full gesun-cycle." That was the length of a day and night on the planet Geheri, the Toth homeworld, the standard of the galaxy. "We might not even need to sleep out there if we get to the ship easily."

"It's important for your client? Why can't he cough up more credits then?"

"Is it money? How much do you want?"

He swallowed suddenly, looking me up and down. Then he took a step back, looked down at the table, and picked up his glass of ale. He took a long swig of it and wiped at his furry upper lip. He named an astronomical amount of credits.

"What?" I said, horrified.

"Yeah, and I want you to sign some affidavit or something that if I lose it out there and rape you, you're not going to get me locked up."

My mouth went dry. He just *said* that. "That's a real concern?"

"You still want to go?"

"I can never get that amount of credits."

"Contact your client," he said, taking another drink of ale. "See what he says. You know where to find me."

"I… there's no way," I said.

He gave me an easy grin, backing away with another shrug.

I went after him. I took him by the arm to stop him, and I pulled him in close.

Okay, bad idea. Because, whoa, I could smell him, and he smelled… well, not like anything, not like… I don't know, like *sex*, but in a good way, like some very earthy and very hot kind of something that seemed to burst inside my nostrils and set up this chain reaction that went to my breasts and between my thighs, and I twitched all over.

He sucked in a breath, yanking out of my grasp.

I'd somehow spoken at the same time. My intent with pulling him in close had been to whisper this to him, and so I'd said it. "I'm with the resistance."

So, I didn't know why he pulled away. Was it because of what I'd said or because of… did he smell that I…? *Stars.*

His gaze found mine.

"Please," I said. "It's important that I get to that ship."

He shook his head slowly. "There isn't a resistance anymore," he said, his voice barely audible.

I shrugged, spreading my hands. "Nothing too centralized, no. For fear of being crushed. But we never really went away, no matter what the Toth say."

"That's…" He scratched the side of his neck. "No way, shei, no way. You just made the whole thing even more dangerous. I'm not sticking my nose out into… I leave the Toth alone, they leave me alone, right? Not getting mixed up in *that*."

Stars.

He backed away again, shaking his head. "Sorry, shei." His voice was louder. "You'll have to wait until after the season."

TWO

cypra

Back in the room I was staying in, one of the local bungalows that functioned like hotels, I was propped up against the headboard of the bed, looking at a holographic image of my current contact with the resistance, a woman named Sienne Dlach. She wasn't a boss or a handler or anything, but she was the person I talked to. There was very little in the way of centralization with the resistance, so messages were often delivered by use of a chain of people, and always orally, never in text form. There were also layers of security that needed to be set up in order to make sure the messages weren't recorded.

Sienne had warm brown skin and short curly black hair. She was a human like me, and she was married to a ccael, which was a species of alien who had a mess of tentacles. They'd actually given me a ride to Ohkk. If I got what I was looking for, they'd probably pick me up again at the rendezvous point.

But considering I wasn't going to get it, I was going to need a ship to come get me sooner, I thought.

"Get a guide of a different species," said Sienne.

"No other species go up there," I said. "I guess those vvoln are scary as all fuck and the only reason anyone went up there was to mate."

She considered. "Well, how necessary is a guide at all?"

"I just said the vvoln were scary," I said.

"You know how to use a blaster, though, right?"

I nodded. "Sure."

"And you can program the coordinates into a speeder," she said. "You just go up there on your own."

I sucked in a breath. It was dangerous, of course, but everything about being in the resistance was danger. "That's what you think I should do? I was thinking… you know how sometimes women volunteer to do those longterm spy arrangements where they have to, like, infiltrate the Toth by posing as sex workers? By, um, by *being* sex workers?"

"Uh, yeah, but that's a volunteer thing," said Sienne. "I would never volunteer for that."

"Maybe this would kind of be the same thing, though," I said. "I have to fuck this guy, you know, for the cause." I squared my shoulders.

She raised her eyebrows. "How long has it *been?*"

"That's not the point."

"What does he *look* like?"

I blushed. "That's also not the point." I shook my head. "Anyway, it doesn't matter. He won't do it. He wants more credits than anyone could ever get him for the job." I didn't tell her I'd broken cover. That was a bad thing to have done, and it wouldn't go over well.

"I thought you said it was like an out-of-control thing, anyway. Sounds…" She considered. "I don't know. Maybe from a certain perspective, I could see the kink factor there, but overall, no, it sounds insanely dangerous."

"Well, so is going up there on my own with a speeder and a blaster," I said.

"If he ruts out or whatever, I'm guessing he's going to be useless against those vvoln things, so then you'll be in the exact same place as you are now. No, worse, because they'll be coming for you, and he'll have you pinned down with his—"

"Okay, seriously, Sienne, I just said he'd never do it. I really don't have any options. I have to go out there on my own."

"You don't have to do anything," said Sienne. "If this is too much for you, we'll assign someone else."

"Yeah, and I'll have to find my own way off the planet," I said. The resistance was strictly voluntary, but I'd been in so long that I depended on them for transportation and funds. They didn't so much pay as they just bought me food and places to sleep and that sort of thing. Maybe if I was that dependent on them, it wasn't strictly voluntary, but it didn't matter.

The Toth needed to be stopped, and I was going to do my part.

Back only a generation ago, things were very, very bad in this galaxy for humans. The Toth lost all their women to a weird virus and they bred with humans instead, but not in a nice, respectful way. In an abduction-sex-slave way. In a we-think-all-other-species-besides-us-are-basically-animals-even-as-we're-using-them-for-reproduction way. The Toth took us from our homeworld, Earth, which is in another galaxy, and used to be easily reachable through a wormhole in space. Except that closed up, and now, we humans in this galaxy were just stuck here. It was fine with me.

I'd never been to Earth. My grandmothers were both abducted, and so this galaxy had always been my home.

Sometimes, you heard stories from other humans

about Earth, how it was so much better there. But what did it matter? We couldn't get there, so we needed to make *this* galaxy better.

Both of my grandmothers were bred by the Toth after they arrived, so I had half-Toth relatives somewhere, I guessed. Sometimes Toth let the human mothers stay with their kids. Lots of times, though, once they decided they were done with the humans, they dumped them. I grew up in the Colony, this humans-only settlement on Jenthe. It's a desert planet, but the little area where the humans live is an oasis, and it's nice there. Sort of. I mean, it's hard to escape the fact that no matter what, you're living in a prison, basically. I had to get out of there.

There's lots of ways out for a human girl in the Colony, but most of them involve selling your body for sex in one way or the other. The Toth rule the galaxy. We humans are very similar to Toth. The basic differences are just that the Toth have no hair and that their skin color ranges all over, instead of the muted sort of tones humans tend to have. Toth will be bright green or pale purple, that kind of thing. Anyway, they only wanted to breed with us, and it's a known fact that if the ruling class of a society wants something, then the people in the lower classes covet it, too.

These days, the Toth have a whole generation of half-Toth women and they are steadily trying to breed out all the human characteristics, so they don't want humans anymore.

And *everything* else does.

Maybe I shouldn't actually say the first thing. The Toth maybe didn't want to breed us anymore, but they seemed to have developed some kind of sexual fetish for us. Witness the prevalence of Toth-human porn, as

Holston referenced.

Well, there was lots of human porn in general—human girls with every species you could think of.

Anyway, I could have gotten off Jenthe easily enough if I wanted to trade sex for credits and freedom. But I chose the resistance instead. Maybe, though, it was that prevalent attitude in the galaxy towards human women that made me think it wouldn't be that big of a deal to just spread my thighs for Holston.

Or maybe it really had been too long since I got laid.

"Caspe and I can probably come get you," Sienne was saying. "This assignment, it's insane."

"But we need those schematics," I said. It was a new ion cannon that the Toth had just created. If we had all of the digital files on how to make one, we could use it to know their weaknesses and to create our own weapons against the Toth. It really was important, and I didn't take this assignment lightly.

"Maybe," she said. "It just seems like they should have sent someone else."

"I can handle it," I said.

"You're all alone," she said. "I don't like it. Look, maybe Caspe and I should come anyway. Have you seen what Caspe can do with his tentacles? This one time, he and I were in this abandoned lab on Geheri—"

"You were on the Toth homeworld? Was this for the resistance?"

"Um, no, it was before that. Not the point. The point is, he's pretty lethal when he needs to be, and whatever these vvoln things are, I think—"

"I can handle it," I said. "You guys have your own mission."

"At least let me send a message up the chain about your situation," she said.

"No, don't worry about it." I took a deep breath. "I'll figure it out. I can handle it."

"Saying that ten times is not going to make it actually true."

"Sure it is." I grinned at her.

She shook her head, laughing. "Okay, okay, fine. I'll do nothing, then. And we really are on our way to the other side of the galaxy, so it wouldn't be easy to get back to you. Even so, you say the word, and we'll turn around."

"I don't need that."

"If you do, though?"

"Sure, if I do," I said. "But I won't."

* * *

holston

I sipped the rest of my drink in the corner, sitting alone, feeling off balance.

So, that was a human female, huh?

Well, then.

Obviously, when you were part of a species that only got aroused sexually on a seasonal basis anyway, sex was a completely different proposition than if you were like the Toth, who could go anytime. Well, lots of species were like that, opportunistic breeders. The seasonal thing was not necessarily the norm. The fact that our species survived so long being that way and getting pulverized by the predators that decimated us every mating season was kind of crazy when I thought about it.

Nature finds a way, that's the thing. Nature is tenacious.

Anyway, the point was, there were a lot of donen who were sort of jealous of the anatomy of everything else out there. They'd take synthetic stimulants designed to make them aroused outside of the seasonal paradigm just to experience the whole thing.

It sounded insane to me. Complicated. Expensive, because it involved buying the stimulants and then usually paying someone for sex, also. It'd be one thing if you fell in love with some woman who wasn't a donen, I guess. It went without saying that women of our own species were usually not particularly down with indulging this whole thing with donen males who were trying to compete with the Toth or whatever.

That was for two reasons, I guess.

One was that women as a whole tended not to do ridiculous things just to get laid. I don't know if it was just that—for a woman—the whole prospect of sex was dangerous enough without taking even *more* risks or if it was because they could be satisfied without triggering our mating cocks at all.

Maybe a little of both.

Donen men couldn't mate if they weren't in a rut, because our bodies sucked our penises and scrotum inside a cavity in our pelvises and they didn't come out until we were properly stimulated. We did have another protuberance, which was called a pleasure cock in typical slang. It was under our fur. It was flat and long and kind of rounded at the end, and it could come out on its own. It got engorged, but not, uh, erect.

Like mine? Mine responded to that human girl.

Crazy response, actually.

I'd never felt anything like that.

But I'd never been around a woman who wasn't on some kind of mating suppressant either, and humans, they had short gemoonthly cycles, and she could be... opportunistic breeders, I mean...

We were compatible with humans.

Humans were *crazy* compatible. Almost anything could knock up a human girl.

I don't know how it would work though.

With our species, if we did anything naturally, which we didn't, it was supposed to work like this:

Step One, the season came on, making everyone horny, making both males and females release pheromones and triggering typical mating behavior, which included receptiveness in females and aggressiveness in males—the aggressiveness was for the mating behavior, but it was also against other males.

Step Two, a receptive female got caught by an aggressive male who mounted her so that his pleasure cock would stimulate her clitoris, triggering her ovulation cycle.

Step Three, the mating cock emerged. Second mounting occurred, sometime after the first. Sometimes, I thought, back in the day, it wouldn't even be the same guy, because while he was waiting around to fuck her, he either got killed or some other guy stole her from him or whatever.

Step Four, constant mounting and fucking in some area the male could protect from predators and other men who were coming to try and steal his mate from him. Lots more chances of everyone *dying*.

Then, of course, once the rut was done, there was the danger of getting the whole herd back from the region near the pole where mating was done, and the vvoln probably took out a bunch of pregnant women every cycle.

To survive as long as we did under these conditions, we must have had a lot of babies was all I could think. Every single female must have gotten knocked up every cycle. We did have a tendency for multiples in litters, actually. Two or three wasn't uncommon, but nowadays women took things to suppress aspects of their ovulation also, keep it down to one egg at a time.

So, with a human girl, I didn't know. She didn't need me to trigger her ovulation.

Me?

Er, a man.

Not me.

Of course, the way that a pleasure cock triggered ovulation was through giving a woman an orgasm. I *could* do that to her. I knew lots about female human anatomy. Porn, right?

Not that I looked at that shit regularly.

I mean, I didn't get the point. I was on suppressants. I didn't want to be a daddy anytime soon. I didn't *think* about sex.

Why would I?

Okay, I mean... everyone thinks about sex sometimes, but I didn't get...

The pleasure cock didn't ejaculate or anything, but it was capable of its own sort of climax, a peak point of pleasure that culminated in a pulsing sensation in the pleasure cock, and if I wanted to look at porn and masturbate, I mean... that's what I'd be stroking.

I knew there were donen men who seemed to be obsessed with doing that kind of thing, like... I didn't know, I guess people could get addicted to anything pleasurable, and orgasms are that, so it made sense. It was just that I didn't do that.

I couldn't even remember the last time I masturbated, and when I did, I definitely did not look at human porn. Truthfully, I sneered at that kind of thing. It seemed like a Toth thing, wanting human girls, especially when we had our own women and when we—unlike the Toth—had no problem with reproduction. We had to suppress our reproduction because it was too effective and prolific. If we did reproduce at a rate that was "natural" we'd need predators to eat us or else we'd outgrow our planet. So, I didn't know, I just didn't see the point in getting all obsessed with sex, really.

I never thought about it.

I was belaboring this point, but she….

The way she *smelled*…

Fuck.

I sat there, nursing my drink and feeling uncomfortably aroused, my pleasure cock twitching away under my fur every time I thought about her. I kept having to sort of rearrange myself because it was trying to nudge itself out.

Embarrassing.

People came over and tried to talk to me, but I just shook my head at them and told them I wasn't up to conversation at the time. I wasn't exactly what you'd call a social person. I did see people but I'd often go out and live in the wild, no other person around at all, and be out there, just living off the land for gemoons. So, people were used to my crotchety behavior and they cleared out, thinking I was just being me.

I kept thinking my stupid pleasure cock was going to go *down*. And that then I could get up and walk out easily, without worrying that it was going to be peeking out and that I was going to be indecent.

I kept thinking that I'd stop scenting like a horny gratts, and then I could get closer to people.

Neither of these happened, so eventually, I skulked out of the bar.

I scented the human girl.

I knew it was stupid to follow the scent. I knew it was probably also creepy, possibly even criminal. What did I think I was going to do? Track her to wherever she was sleeping? Watch her through the window? Sneak inside to get closer? Nah, maybe I'd do the super classy thing and just crouch somewhere in the shadows and rub one out while I was close to her scent. That wasn't positively *disgusting*.

I…

I knew men did things like that. Usually not donen men, but men of other species, and I'd always thought it was gross and baffling, and now I entirely understood it, entirely.

I'd been around humans before.

Never a woman, admittedly.

I wondered if everyone was reacting to her this way. She said she'd talked to some other potential guides. What if she went back to one of them? What if he agreed to take her up to the pole?

I sucked in a breath at that.

So, I'm possessive of her, too?

Seriously?

I was terrified. I was out of control, and I'd never felt like this in my entire life, never. I knew that the intelligent thing to do would be to turn around, go home, scrub her scent off in the shower, take a sleeping pill, and forget all about that human woman.

There was a spirit in our mythology, a woman-shaped thing who also had antlers—I don't know what that was about, to be honest, but I found it kind of hot, and I didn't know if that meant I had latent homosexual desires, which I knew I was supposed to be cool with but which always gave me this prick of something like a rush of hot fear, right up my spine, something I couldn't fight, something that maybe made the whole thing hotter, disturbingly—and the spirit would lure unsuspecting men out of their homes and away from their families, typically to their death.

She was called an ulin.

That's what this human was. An ulin sent to *destroy* me by the mischievous, ancient spirits of the land.

Yeah, I didn't believe in any of that, of course, but I really should stay away from her.

I told myself this the whole time I was following her scent, all the way until I was at the string of little bungalows, even when I got right up on the one that smelled like her.

But before I could look in the window or go off somewhere and start playing with myself like some kind of criminal deviant, I made myself go to her door, and I banged on it.

She opened it, and she was less clothed than the last time, in this little dress-shirt thing that didn't even reach her knees. She peered at me with her smooth, pale skin and her jet black hair, which she had cut short, as was the style, but which fringed out over her forehead, shimmering in the lights. "Oh, stars, it's you. I thought you were someone who worked here, coming to ask about the fan and I was going to say it's working again, and I was..." Her words trailed off. "You want to come inside?"

Come inside? She just *said* that. Great. My pleasure cock heard that.

Fuck.

"I'm good," I said. "Just talk through the doorway here."

"Okay," she said, and she looked down at her bare

legs and her utter lack of clothing and grimaced.

What was I even doing here? I folded my arms over my chest. My voice came out gruff. "You got any other interest in this? Someone else who's offering to go up there with you?"

"I *told* you," she said. "Everyone said that the only person stupid enough to do it would be *you*." Then she winced. "I mean, I'm not saying you're stupid—"

"What are the coordinates?" I said, lifting one hand, the one with my bracelet.

"Oh, um..." She pulled up her own bracelet and pulled up a holoprojection which beamed up out of the top of it. She read the coordinates to me.

I dutifully inputted them and then sighed. "We could get maybe halfway by speeder, but there's only an ancient, falling-down footbridge over this river here." I turned my bracelet so that she could see the holoproj of the map that I was looking at. I jabbed a finger into the river in question.

"A hover speeder?" she said. They could go over water.

"Nah, never make it," I said. "They're all solar powered and there's no light up there."

"Right," she said with a sigh. "So, it's hopeless?"

"Well, look, if we go this way..." I traced a route with my finger, "we can go around the river and we can get the speeder up there but it'll take days. We'll have to camp out there. If we have a speeder, it should be safe enough. The vvoln won't be able to get inside, and we can sleep inside it."

"Are you going to do it? Are you going to take me?" She gave me a big smile.

"I shouldn't," I said.

"Look, I really can't get you that money," she said. "I

would if I had any access to funds, but I actually—"

"It *is* stupid," I said, looking her over. My gaze settled on the place where her shirt hit her bare thighs. Our women didn't have legs like humans did, and I would have sworn to you that I didn't even like their smooth, bare skin there, that I preferred a woman with solid, furred legs and hooves. I would have said that humans' legs looked breakable and weak and exposed, like larvae, like hairless spawns of rodents, like...

I was a liar, though, because they were mesmerizing, her thighs, the way they were shaped, the curves of them, the way they met her knees, every aspect of them completely on display. I... there was maybe nothing more erotic in the *galaxy* than the look of the swell of her calves.

She noticed me noticing and she pressed her thighs together.

My pleasure cock tried to push its way out behind the fur on my crotch again and I shifted position, lowered my arms, covering myself by putting clasped hands in front of myself and forcing my gaze upward to meet hers.

Her lips were parted, and the tighter she squeezed her thighs together the headier her scent was, a musk of undeniable arousal.

My jaw tightened. "This isn't like me," I said, echoing what I'd said to her earlier.

"Me either," she whispered.

"I shouldn't take you up there," I said. The bottom had gone out of my voice. "I should probably stay away from you. This is... this is..."

"But you're going to, anyway?" She bit down on her bottom lip.

I swallowed. "Has anyone else... any of the other

donen men you've interacted with, have they… reacted to you—"

"No, just you," she said. She sounded out of breath at that. "And this reaction, my reaction, it's only for you, too. I don't…"

I furrowed my brow. Well, that blew my little theory of human girls breaking through my suppressants, didn't it? I reached up to run a finger over the tip of one of my antlers. "Huh."

"Are you going to help me get to the ship?"

"Yeah," I said. "I am." *And, uh, I don't want you too far away from me either due to this weird, inexplicable possessive thing I have developed.* "You on Geheri time?" Geheri was the Toth home planet, and all units of measurement, including time, tended to be predicated on it.

"No?" She was confused.

"I just mean that this planet is much smaller than Geheri, so the day and night cycle is really short, and usually we sleep either every second or third night, depending, and the frequent short sleep cycles aren't always easy for offworlders who are used to sleeping for long periods of time, like a whole Geheri night."

"No, I'm acclimated," she said. "I've been looking for you for at least seven of these planet's days, and I am tired now, but—"

"We should go once the sun comes up," I said. "You should sleep at my place."

Her eyebrows shot up.

"I have guest rooms," I said. "But it'll be easier. We can get moving more quickly that way. I won't… I swear I'm not going to…" I squirmed. "Touch you."

"I paid for this—"

"Yeah, well, I'm—"

"I'll be more comfortable here on my own," she said.

"You want me to take you up to the pole, we do this my way." I tried to look intimidating and insistent, which is tough when you have your hands folded in front of your crotch, holding your pleasure cock from springing out.

She let out a disbelieving noise. "I would have to pack everything up."

"Well, that's my point," I said. "Better to do it now than to slow us down in the morning."

She tilted her head to one side, accepting this. "Fine." She shut the door in my face. "Let me get dressed." Her voice was muffled by the door.

"Yeah," I said. I tucked my pleasure cock all the way back, shoving it away, smoothing my fur over it, swearing inwardly. What the fuck was wrong with me, anyway?

She yanked the door open. Now, she was wearing a pair of pants and she had a big bag slung over her shoulder. She raised her eyebrows at me.

"That was fast," I said.

She shrugged. "I packed light." She tilted her head again. "So, I guess I would have been able to get ready quickly in the morning?" It was pointed.

I cleared my throat, shifting on my hooves. "This way." I walked down off the steps.

She caught up with me, on her bracelet, fingers moving over the holoproj.

"What are you doing?"

"Checking out of the bungalow where I'm no longer staying," she said. "Which I'm going to be charged for, regardless of where I sleep at this point."

"Sorry," I said, gruff.

"It's fine. It'll be covered," she said.

Right, by the resistance. The second reason why it was incredibly stupid to be helping this girl out. "The people in the ship, were they rebels too?" I said.

"Not so loud," she admonished, looking around.

"Sorry," I said. "Actually, let's not talk about that."

"Fine," she said.

We didn't end up talking at all. It took about twenty hidosecs to walk to my place, and half of that was the driveway. I had managed to get a bunch of land out here cheap a few years back, and then I'd built this place over time. Not with my bare hands or anything. I wasn't worthless with a hammer, though. I *could* build things, but I tended to stick to my own skill set. It was more that I hired people for little modular areas of the thing, and I added to it in sections.

When it came into view around one of the bends, she sucked in a breath. "Wow."

"Uh, it's not really finished," I muttered. It was designed to blend into the scenery, made of natural-looking materials, built in between the trees. And it was kind of sprawling at this point. I didn't know why I'd built so much onto it. I guessed I figured eventually I was going to want to go off the suppressants and breed some woman and make babies or something. Like, not yet, but someday.

I was scared of doing that, of course, but it'd probably be cool, teaching my kids about the outdoors, how to camp and fish and hunt and hike and all of that?

"It's gorgeous," she said.

"It's nothing," I said. Why was I embarrassed by her compliments? The truth was I never brought people here. The truth was, I was not a very social person.

"It's not nothing," she insisted. "I love that part up

there. Is that built *around* the tree?"

"Yeah, it's..." I started that way, and we went up the spiral staircase that was built around the tree to climb up to the little room up here. "This is a guest room now, actually," I said. "I was thinking I was going to make it my room, but I never got it together enough to pack up my other bedroom. There's a bathroom through here." I opened a door to show her. "You'll be comfortable here?"

"Seriously?" She was looking around the room, which wasn't really well furnished or decorated or anything. I had gotten a bed for it, but I didn't really know why. There were four guest rooms in this house, and I told myself I was going to have people over. Have a big thing with food or something? Maybe I'd sit out on one of my porches playing my huuq, which was a stringed instrument from the planet Bothora that I'd picked up on a whim at some point. I wasn't very good, but I liked to mess around with it from time to time.

Of course, I never did this.

I didn't even know who I'd ask.

I knew people, but not people who were close enough friends to invite over like that.

"I get to stay *here?*" She grinned at me. "I love this place. I love everything about it. Oh, man, if I lived here, I would never leave."

I rubbed the back of my neck, embarrassed. "It's isolated and peaceful, which I like."

"It's beautiful." She peered out the windows. This circular room up here was surrounded by windows, and there were inner windows as well, so that the tree trunk it was built around was visible. "The sun comes up over there?"

"Yeah," I said. "If you want the windows dimmed,

there's a switch—"

"In about four hihors?"

"Yeah," I said. "About that."

"Well, I guess I should get some rest, if we're off with the dawn." She was still grinning.

"Uh... yeah." Now, I had to leave her here. I was thinking that I might sleep in a different room myself tonight, one that was closer to the base of this tree, so that if anyone tried to get to her, I'd be able to—

What was wrong with me?

I left her and forced myself to go back to my own room, where I searched on my bracelet for things like, *Human scent and donen mating suppressant failure.*

But this only led me to a search result that said, *Frequently forgetting your mating suppressant? Switch to daily pills.*

Forgetting?

Shit.

I took once-a-gemoon pills that I was reminded to take by a reminder set on my bracelet, but some people couldn't remember to take the suppressants if they were so spread out and preferred taking one pill a day so that it could be a routine. I'd never forgotten one. Never once.

But when I went to my medicine cabinet and took out my little blister pack of pills, there it was. The one I should have taken a fogemoon ago? Right freaking there.

I groaned, popped it out, and swallowed it.

So, this was why I was reacting like this to her. It had nothing to do with her being human and everything to do with the fact that I hadn't had a suppressant in so long that it had entirely worn off. I guessed that I hadn't noticed before now because all the women I tended to interact with were similarly suppressed and that human woman was probably fertile or something.

Humans were fertile a ridiculous amount of the time, after all, like six gesuns out of every gemoon or something, twelve times a gecycle. Donens could get pregnant once during our planet's cycle around our sun, which translated to twice a gecycle—a gecycle was a circuit around Geheri's sun.

Then I searched on my bracelet for what happened if I took the suppressant late. How soon would it kick in?

The good news was that it should start working within two or three gesuns.

The bad news was that if I went up to the poles where the plants were that triggered my mating instincts and I got worked up, they might not kick in at all.

I traced a finger over my antlers.

Well, lose me in deep space. This wasn't good.

THREE

cypra

I'd barely gotten to sleep when there was a knock on the door of the room where I was staying. I had to admit that this cool treehouse room was a step up from that nasty bungalow I'd been sleeping in. The windows were open, giving a cool breeze, and the fan in here was superior. I was actually not sweating, which was maybe a first for being on this planet.

I got up.

He'd already seen me in my nightgown, after all.

I opened the door. "Everything okay?" I stifled a yawn.

"Sorry to wake you, I just… I shouldn't take you up there."

I yawned again. "You've said this before."

"I, uh, I realized this, uh, this *way* I've been acting with you, it's because I forgot to take my suppressant pill. I guess you're probably fertile or something and it triggered me in some way. I realized it, and I took it, but I read up on it, and if I go up to the pole, my suppressant might not kick in."

I blinked at him. "I'm not fertile, trust me. I have an implant."

"Well, whatever," he said. "It doesn't matter. The point is, it wouldn't be right for me to take you up there."

"You said before if I just signed an affidavit that I wouldn't care if you lost control and raped me, it would be fine." I yawned again. *Oh, now I'm saying that word like it's nothing.*

His nostrils flared.

I shrugged. "We're attracted to each other. Right?"

"I'm just off my suppressant. I'd be attracted to anything right now."

I pressed my lips together. Well, fuck him, too. "I'm just saying…"

"What are you saying?" He looked me over. "You're saying, you, uh, you *want…*" He couldn't finish the sentence. His voice had gotten very hoarse.

"No one else is going to take me up to the pole. You're all I have," I said. "And I'm really willing to do whatever it takes to complete this mission. It's important. So, I can handle it."

He touched the tip of one of his antlers, pressing his finger into it in a way that was making me nervous. I was afraid he was going to break the skin, hurt himself, but I guess he could tell that wouldn't happen. How sharp were the tips of them anyway? "I'll, uh, I'll stay in control of myself."

"That's a thing you can do?"

He sighed. "Go back to sleep." He backed away, heading back down the stairs.

"We're still leaving in the morning then?" I called after him.

"First thing, shei," he called back.

I shut the door and climbed back into bed. His house was really cool. He was… I liked him. I probably shouldn't, because he was kind of rude and he was really pushy and he seemed to think he had the right to boss me around. On paper, actually, this guy was not even remotely likable.

Maybe it was just his lack of suppressant?

He was probably giving off some crazy male pheromone thing to make me receptive to his mating advances.

He'd said the thing about how humans pretended we couldn't smell things, and I couldn't deny that he smelled *great*.

Maybe this was all just a bunch of chemical stuff that would wear off once his suppressant started working again.

Of course, he'd just said that it might not work if we went up to the pole.

So, that would mean...

I rolled over in bed and grabbed my bracelet to look up donen mating.

I read and read and read, eyes widening.

* * *

cypra

I had planned on renting a speeder, but Holston said we should take his, because it was made specifically for traveling off road, and there weren't a lot of roads up there. It was a big thing, with four huge tires with deep treads, and we had to climb up built-in ladders to get in. Inside, I looked around at the two-person sitting area and couldn't figure out how we were both going to sleep in this thing like he'd said we would.

We were going to be on top of each other. Of course, what with all I'd read about donen mating habits, it wasn't a particularly tender thing that happened organically from being in each other's arms. It was more of a chasing-down-and-pinning-against-a-tree-trunk thing.

So, maybe it didn't matter in the end.

I also was not going to admit to myself that my stomach did this funny flipping over thing at the thought of being pinned to a tree trunk by Holston or anything like that either, because…

Well, better not to acknowledge, really.

He seemed to have taken a page out of the same book this morning and was barely looking at me. When we spoke, we were both businesslike. We ate a quick breakfast of protein ration bars and talked only about what route we'd take up to the pole.

Then we climbed up into the speeder and I looked around and thought about how we couldn't sleep in there and said nothing to him about that.

We strapped in to the seats. He drove.

We took off.

It was early morning, but we went due north, and within about two hihors, it looked as if dusk was settling.

For another hihor, we kept pacing with the setting sun, so it was sort of perpetually going down. Of course, you couldn't quite see it, not through the heavy atmosphere that was settled over the planet. It was beautiful, though, the way that the sun reflected against the clouds, staining everything bright colors—a range of reds, purples, oranges, and fuchsias.

Then we burst out of the clouds and into the darkness.

Overhead, the sky was pitch black, dotted in stars, and everything felt a little less humid but somehow warmer. I started sweating again, and I asked about putting on the climate control in the speeder and Holston growled that it was a waste of fuel and I opened the window instead.

He turned to glare at me, his antlers brushing against the ceiling and I told him to watch the road.

"Put up the window," he said, flipping on the climate control.

"But—"

"Last thing I need is pollen from the plants," he said pointedly.

Oh, right. That would make him pin me to a tree trunk. I was intrigued by the fact that his kind had two different appendages down there, one literally called an arousal protuberance by the scientific-sounding articles I'd read. Apparently, their women had to have an orgasm in order to ovulate, and that kicked off the entire process, and I was extremely interested in the fact donen males had an entire organ whose only purpose was to get their partners off.

I wanted to see it.

I'd tried to look for pictures on my bracelet last night—yes, I should have been sleeping and I meant to sleep, I just... Anyway, there had been none, only things behind paywalls. Apparently, there was a distinct lack of easily accessible donen pornography, probably owing to the fact that they'd been suppressing themselves unless they actually wanted to have kids, which meant that donen sexual interest was apparently pretty low.

That seemed sad to me, though.

Sex was a part of life, and jettisoning one's desire for it seemed...

Of course, what was I saying? I never thought much about sex either. But that was just because I was busy and I had other things to occupy me. I could get horny if I wanted. Witness this now.

Except *had* I chosen this?

I closed the window.

We continued driving. We were now traversing a narrow road that was made of dirt. It had big ruts, and the big wheels of the speeder bounced over them. It was a jolting ride. It was dark, no lights except the frontlamps of the speeder illuminating the path directly in front of us.

We crested over a hill, and there was something in the road.

"Lose me in deep space!" exclaimed Holston, slamming on the brakes.

We screeched to a stop.

Now, halted, I could see that it was a huge animal of some kind, all covered in dark fur. It was taking up the entire road.

"Can we go around?" I said.

"I'm not sure we'll clear those trees." Holston gestured, and I could see that on either side of the road there were trees, too close. "Shit." He threw open the door to the speeder and climbed down.

I followed suit.

Holston walked around the front of the thing. I followed him.

And then recoiled, letting out a little noise. The front of the creature was a mess of gore. Its face and front had been removed, leaving a red-smeared rib cage jutting out.

Long ropes of bloody guts were strewn out in a line from the body, a macabre path leading off the road. The fur of the animal was blood spattered.

"Shei, maybe you should go back up into the speeder," said Holston.

"I'm fine," I said. "I've seen it now." I was defensive, but it was pretty gross, and I wasn't honestly used to seeing this kind of carnage. "What did this?"

"What do you think?" he said.

"A vvoln?" I cringed. "How big are vvoln?"

Holston laughed.

I hunched up my shoulders. This animal was enormous. It looked as though it would have been as big as our speeder if it hadn't been half eaten.

"Predators can take down prey bigger than themselves," said Holston. "Vvoln aren't as big as these guys—this is a jurrn—but they're big enough." He gestured with his hand to indicate chest level. "About this tall. Go on all fours. They have tusks."

"Yeah, I looked at some pictures on my bracelet." Great, my voice was trembling.

"Go into the speeder," said Holston.

"What are you going to do?" I said. "You can't move this thing."

"It's mostly hollow, shei," he said. "I'll just drag it off."

"I'll help you," I said stoutly.

He snorted.

"I can help," I said, insistent now. "Look, we'll each get a leg." I went over and found one of its legs and wrapped my arms around it and tugged. It *was* mostly hollow, and I was surprised at how light it was. I was able to drag it by myself.

"Shei, I got it," he said.

I let go of it. "I guess you probably don't need help," I decided and backed away.

He took over, tugging on the carcass. He pulled on it, and it sort of folded in on itself, collapsing.

I recoiled again, this time from the splatter of blood. Luckily, I wasn't close enough that any got on me.

He grunted, pulling harder, except this collapse

meant that the animal ripped in half, and there was a tearing noise, and more blood—

Eew.

I turned away, grimacing. I was embarrassed, but *gross.*

When I turned back, he'd gotten half the animal off the road and he was walking back towards the speeder. "Come on," he said.

"But, the rest of it—"

"We can get around the rest of it," he said.

Oh, of course. I climbed back up into the speeder, and I felt gross from where I'd touched the dead animal's leg. Did I smell like it? I sniffed, trying not to let on that was what I was doing.

He noticed anyway and laughed at me.

I glowered at him.

"We'll camp up near the bend in the river," he said. "You can take a nice bath and wash away anything you got on yourself."

"A bath in a river?" I blinked at him.

He laughed again. "Or not."

"Well, it's not time to camp yet," I said. "Right?"

"No, we're not even close to the river," he said.

And then we settled into silence again.

FOUR

holston

I was monitoring myself so much for signs that my suppressant was working or that it wasn't that I couldn't tell. I'd think to myself that it must be working, because I was fine, and then she'd shift in the speeder and I'd get flooded with her scent, and my pleasure cock would get all excited and I'd realize I was still definitely affected.

But was it worse than before or just the same?

I kept trying to convince myself it wasn't worse.

But I worried that it was, and so that made me more attuned to every little sensation I felt.

When we finally stopped to camp, I was glad, because at least I'd have other things to focus on besides her and the way she was affecting me. I even decided that we should have food, real food, not just those ration bars, because that would give me something to do.

I could have brought a blaster with me, but I didn't tend to carry them, as a general rule. A blaster would be too loud, and besides, I didn't like to scorch perfectly good bits of meat with the thing. We wanted something small to eat, like a bird, and there was no reason to waste half of it with a blaster.

So, instead, I had a bolts and bow, and I got that out

of the speeder.

Cypra saw me climbing down with it, and she was wary, but I explained to her it was just for dinner.

"You can go and wash in the river, if you want," I said. "That way, I won't be near you. Safer that way."

"Well, depending on your perspective," she said.

"Look, you see a vvoln, just yell," I said. "I'll be close. I'll come right back."

She shook her head. "I've seen this holovid, okay, and I'm not going to be that dumb girl who takes all her clothes off in the woods."

My pleasure cock twitched. "I figured, uh, you bathe first, and I hunt, and then while the food is cooking, I would bathe. So, we're both going to be dumb, and it's going to be fine. I come out here all the time."

"You go on and on about those predators, and it's fine?"

"Well, *I'm* going in the river before we bed down in the speeder," I said.

"I'll do it when you do it," she said, lifting her chin.

My mouth was dry. "That seems…"

"I know, but it's dark, and I'm way more afraid of having my insides eaten out like that jurrn than I am of you, you know, forcing me to have an orgasm with your arousal protuberance."

My pleasure cock swelled. "Well," I muttered, "someone's been doing some reading."

She folded her arms over her chest.

"You can get naked while I'm there to protect you, shei." I took off into the woods, taking my weapon. "Hunting now."

"I'll just stay in the speeder, then," she called after me.

"Great," I called back.

In the woods, I stared up at the tree branches crisscrossing against the starry sky and tried to figure out what the fuck I was even doing out here.

It didn't make any sense.

I had every reason not to be out there with her. Taking her out to this ship of hers was dangerous on three different levels. First, we could be eaten by vvoln. Second, I could force myself on her. Third, she was with the resistance, and if anyone found out I helped the resistance, that wasn't going to be good.

I wasn't thinking clearly, which was an obvious sign that the mating instinct in me had taken over to a dangerous degree.

Overhead, a set of dark wings blocked out the sky.

I lifted the bow and fitted a bolt to the notch on it. Pulling back the string, I sighted the bird and let the bolt fly.

It hit home.

The bird plummeted.

I went to catch it.

The bird fell, but it got stuck on a set of branches and leaves overhead. I swung up into the tree—my hooves were better at climbing than other species always seemed to think they would be—and snatched down the bird.

Then I went back to the speeder.

I set up a small cook fire, cleaned the bird, slid it onto a spit, and left it to slowly roast over the flame.

Then I climbed up to the speeder and banged on her window.

She opened it.

"Ready to take your clothes off?" I raised my eyebrows.

She huffed. "You don't have to be awful about it. You're making fun of me, but you've spent all this time trying to convince me it's actually dangerous, and I don't think I'm being unreasonable."

I didn't answer that. I wasn't making fun of her. I was annoyed with her because she was insisting on making this harder for me, that was all. Didn't she get that if I was aroused, I was going to be less effective at taking down vvoln? I climbed down off the speeder.

She came down too.

I walked to the river, glancing over my shoulder now and again to make sure she was coming.

The trees gave way at the bank of the river, though some of their branches hung over, vines dripping off of them in the darkness. The river itself was wide and gleaming, broken here and there by smooth stones. The water moved over them, not too swiftly. It reflected back the brightness of the stars overhead.

I stepped in. Ah, that was nice. It was cool and refreshing. "I'll just wade out here and keep my back turned, all right?"

"Okay," she said, letting out a little breath. She still sounded freaked out.

I waded further into the water. It came about up to my waist, but I ducked down, letting it cover my shoulders. I ducked my head backwards, dunking my antlers, my hair.

I heard her climb into the water behind me.

I didn't turn around.

She sucked in a breath. "Cold," she said. Then, "It's nice, actually."

"Mmm," I said. I ducked my face forward, scrubbing at my growth of hair at my chin.

"You can turn around," she said.

I did.

She was crouched down in the water. It was up to her chin. One of her shoulders came up, bare.

Under the water, my pleasure cock fought entirely free from the fur on my crotch. My breathing went erratic. I turned back around.

"You okay?" she said.

I just grunted. I scrubbed at my arms and moved through the cold water, willing it to make my cock deflate. It did, mostly, and I managed to tuck it away. Then I stood up. "I'm clean," I said, without looking at her. I climbed out of the water.

"Oh, fuck," she said softly. "I should have remembered a towel or something."

"Back at camp," I said. Then I realized. "But that would mean you'd have to hike back entirely uncovered. Being a human is really inconvenient, isn't it?" Even our women didn't tend to wear clothes. They had breasts, obviously, but they were deflated when the women weren't fertile and covered by hair on their chests. Humans had breasts that were always rounded and full, all the time, no matter what.

Sure, I'd noticed hers under her clothing. How could I not? They were just *there.*

"Actually, it is," she said. "You know, what with being abducted by the Toth and forced to bear their children and then—"

"Sorry," I said. "I'll run back and get you a towel."

"Quickly?" she said.

"Yes, quickly," I said.

"Because I'll be all alone here, and—"

"It'll take me hisecs, shei." I scampered off, shaking off droplets of water as I did.

When I got back with the towel, she said, "You really

can go quickly, can't you? You sort of gallop with those hooves." Her voice sounded thick, approving, impressed.

I draped the towel over a tree branch. "Look, I'm going to just..." I gestured. I turned my back and moved away, putting distance between us.

"Thank you," she said in a small voice.

I peered up at the stars, sighing heavily.

Then I tensed. Was that...? I'd been sighing, so I wasn't sure what I'd heard, but—

There.

Again.

A rustling.

Then, I caught sight of the glint of a tusk moving between the trees.

I turned and rushed back to Cypra.

She was out of the water, holding the towel with both hands to dry her back, exposing the entirety of the front of her body—her bare breasts—lose me, they were hairless and round and the tips were dark in the starlight, water running in rivulets down her belly, down to the juncture of her thighs, which was covered in a small bit of hair, there, a pointless amount of hair—

I barreled into her, even as she let out a yip of protest.

I pressed her body backwards, through the underbrush, hiding us both. I flattened myself against her, hand over her mouth to shut her up, and we were right up against a tree trunk.

Her eyes were wide.

I turned away from her, looking over my shoulder.

Just as the vvoln wandered out onto the clearing near the river bank.

It was a full grown vvoln, a female, so its tusks were

a little on the smaller side and so was its head. But it was still muscled and powerful, covered in short bristly fur, with a mouth full of fangs and viciously clawed paws.

It lifted its head, sniffing the air.

Cypra jerked into me.

I turned back to her.

She was terrified. Her eyes were wide.

I leaned in, mouth against one of her ears, voice barely audible. "We're good," I breathed.

She shook her head, indicating she did not think we were good, not at all.

I looked back at the vvoln, which sniffed again and then put its head down and lumbered down the bank toward the water. It lowered its head and began to drink.

I moved my hand away from Cypra's mouth, willing her to stay quiet as I did so.

She breathed noisily but she didn't make any other sound.

Oh, lose me, her body was up against mine—her *bare* body—her bare *breasts*. They were soft and springy and *perfect.*

It was my turn to let out a noisy breath.

My pleasure cock stirred, and there was nothing between us. It nudged her, *there,* between her thighs.

Her eyes widened.

I winced.

She shut her eyes, squeezing them tight.

I reached between us to push my pleasure cock back, which… in theory seemed like a great idea, but only meant that now my knuckles were touching her between her legs.

She let out a sharp breath, her eyelids jerking open.

"Sorry," I whispered.

She glared at me.

I stopped moving entirely, unsure what to do. So, now, my knuckle was like, between the lips of her, uh, her pussy, and my hand was wrapped around my pleasure cock, and now…

Not good. Not good. None of this was good.

"Holston," she whispered, panic in her voice.

"What?" I whispered back.

She was looking over my shoulder.

I turned.

Oh. The vvoln had stopped drinking and was sniffing the air, looking around, wary.

"Stars," she said, a whisper, but too loud.

"Shh," I said.

She cringed.

The vvoln started for us.

I stayed still, willing her to stay still, willing us to disappear. It wasn't moving quickly, and it was just being exploratory, so it might be fine. On the other hand, if it came too close and scented us, especially with the musk of our arousal in the air, it might decide we were easy prey and charge us.

And if that was the case, I was not equipped to take on a vvoln in a full-on charge. I didn't have any weapons on me, none.

Idiot, what is wrong with you?

That wasn't like me.

The vvoln halted. It sniffed the air, facing us, its body visible through layers of leaves and vegetation, maybe the length of two of me stretched out away from us both.

I willed it to go away. To turn back to the water and forget about us.

It started into the underbrush, thrusting aside branches with its tusks.

Lose me in deep space. I backed away from Cypra.

My pleasure cock was fully engorged, just *there*, but I couldn't worry about her seeing me. Besides, I'd seen all of her secret parts, right? If I wanted to look again, I could turn back and feast my eyes.

I didn't.

I crouched down, head first, and I started for the vvoln.

The vvoln thrust aside another bit of vegetation.

I waited until its head jerked up with the movement of using its tusks, waited until its throat was exposed.

And then I pounced, leaping forward.

My antlers punctured the exposed throat of the beast, going all the way in, blood spurting.

It let out a high-pitched noise of surprise and pain.

I drove my antlers deeper, shutting it *up*.

The vvoln twitched wildly, striking out with its claws—one of them got my shoulder, three deep gouges into my skin. It undulated and writhed and then went still.

"Oh stars," breathed Cypra.

I was out of breath. This was hurting my neck. My antlers were too far in to pull out on their own, so I had to use my hooves for leverage, holding the vvoln carcass away while I extricated myself.

I straightened.

Cypra was cowering against the tree. She had the towel still, somehow, and she was holding it in front of her, bunching it up, covering most of her breasts with her arms, the towel hanging down to cover the juncture of her thighs. But she was all uncovered and pressed together and rounded and juicy and *enticing*.

My whole body jolted. My pleasure cock throbbed.

And deep inside the cavity of my pelvis, I felt something else, something I'd never felt before, something in there, waking up, and it felt *good*.

I let out a little whimper.

"You k-killed it with your antlers," said Cypra, as if this needed narration.

"I wouldn't have," I said. "It's only… if it had decided to attack us, I'd be no match for it, and I couldn't let anything happen to you, so I *had* to."

"No, I agree. You did." She nodded ferociously.

"If it had just been me, if I hadn't been distracted, I could have evaded it."

"It's okay," she said. Her voice was very small. "Isn't it?"

"Uh… they travel in packs," I said. "Family groups, actually. A mated pair will have offspring every cycle, and the children stay with their parents for a long time, sometimes five or six cycles after they're full grown, so the packs can be… there can be a lot of vvoln all together. And they're vicious when they…" I grimaced. "So, when her pack finds her?"

"It's a female?" she said.

I nodded.

"That's the mama?"

"Could be. Or could be a daughter. Either way, they're not going to be pleased when they find her killed. They'll come for us."

"So… like revenge?"

I shrugged.

"They're that smart?" Her voice was growing panicked.

"Well… I don't know. They'll react. They'll scent us. They'll follow the scent. They'll attack. They might have attacked us anyway, no matter what? No way to know. But they wouldn't have been provoked in the first place if I hadn't done it, so..." I shrugged again. "We can't stay here and sleep anymore. We need to move the speeder."

"Oh," she breathed. "Oh."

Her breath made her chest rise and fall, made her breasts rise and fall, made them move in interesting ways, and my gaze settled there and my pleasure cock shuddered.

"Holston," she snapped, fury in her voice.

I lifted my gaze. "Sorry," I muttered. "I'm going to get your clothes." I went around the vvoln carcass and through the underbrush back to the river. I washed my bloody antlers off and washed the gouges in my shoulder, and then I grabbed her clothes, which were hanging over a tree branch. I gathered them up and started to go back for her.

But she was right there. She'd followed me. She was wrapped up in the towel now, but it was way too small and didn't cover much of anything and—

I turned away from her, holding out the clothes.

She snatched them away.

I struggled to tuck my pleasure cock back under my fur.

"So, your, um, your suppressants don't seem to be working." Her voice had a shrill edge.

"Not really, no," I said.

"Is your shoulder okay?"

"I'll be fine," I muttered. "Are you dressed yet?"

"Almost."

It was quiet.

I stood there, with my back to her, until she indicated she was dressed. Then I turned around and I led the way back to the place where the fire was set up. I turned the bird. I threw myself down on the ground next to the fire and began rummaging through a pack I had out here for some bandages.

"What are you doing?" Now, her voice was even more shrill.

I looked up at her. "Uh, bandaging myself?"

"B-but you said we had to move the speeder!"

"Yeah, before we sleep."

"But what if they come for us?"

"They're afraid of fire." I pointed at it.

"So, we're just going to sit here in the woods while they're stalking us and expect this little fire to protect us?" Her voice was very shrill now.

"Tilt your head back and really project your voice there," I said. "I'm sure you can get even *louder* if you try."

"Fuck you." But this was a venomous whisper.

"Sit down." I nodded to the other side of the fire.

She stared at me, shaking her head. Then, I realized her lower lip was starting to tremble. Her eyes were welling up.

I winced. Shit, I did not mean to make her cry—

But she sniffed very hard, bit down on her bottom lip, and it stopped. She sat down hard on the other side of the fire. She was quiet.

"Look, I'm..." I sighed. I made my voice as gentle as possible. "In the best of times, I'm not really good with people."

"No?" she said. "Well, never would have guessed that."

"I'm trying to apologize," I said.

"No, it's fine," she said. "I mean, you saved my life from the big, bad vvoln, I guess. But you also apparently brought down the rage of her pack—"

"We'll move the speeder, our trail will go cold, and that'll be that," I said.

"Okay," she said, letting out a bitter little laugh. "I'm not going to point out that I'm the one who said that getting naked in the river was a bad idea or anything."

I shook my head. "I think I was against the idea of us doing it at the same time," I said. "If you'd just bathed by yourself and then come back to the fire—"

"You neglected to tell me they were afraid of fire."

"What's not afraid of fire?" Now, *my* voice was getting too loud. I gestured at the sky with both hands. "Everything is afraid of fire."

"Oh, okay, Mr. Outdoorsy Hunter Guy," she said. "I guess that's a thing *you* know, but *I* don't know anything about predators in the woods, especially not on this planet!"

"Well, if you don't know things, ask questions."

"How am I supposed to know what to ask?"

I groaned.

She made a tsking noise.

"Just... accept my apology. Can you do that?"

"You're forgiven," she said in a voice dripping with sarcasm.

I huffed.

She let out another bitter laugh.

We were quiet.

"How long until the food is cooked?" she said in a sulky voice.

"Not too long now," I said.

FIVE

cypra

Well, he'd seen me naked now. Looked me over real good, gotten an eyeful. And then we'd been all smushed together against that tree, and his chest had been warm and the feeling of his smooth skin and his crinkly chest hair against my breasts had been kind of amazing, not going to lie.

And then that… that arousal protuberance, whatever it was, it was like a tongue.

I mean, it wasn't wet like a tongue, but it was long and flat, with a rounded edge, and it was flexible, and it could move, and it had molded itself around my labia, and then parted it and a little bit of it had pressed softly in to kiss my clit, and—

Oh.

But that had been all kinds of confusing, what with my being terrified for my life while it was happening. The vvoln were very scary up close.

Then he'd killed the vvoln.

Without a weapon, just with his body.

And that was… I mean… *hot.*

Gross and bloody and terrifying also, though.

It was all very confusing.

That was probably why I spent the rest of the evening snapping at him. I was confused and frustrated, and my body was all worked up, and I didn't know what to do with myself.

The bird he roasted was actually really delicious. It was crispy on the outside, juicy on the inside. It was seasoned only with a bit of salt that he'd brought in one of his packs, but that simplicity seemed to make it even more delicious.

Or maybe food tasted better after an adrenaline-producing event like that.

I wasn't sure.

After we ate, we packed up all the stuff he'd set out for the fire, which wasn't much actually, climbed back in the speeder, and then we drove off.

In the distance, we heard a chorus of wailing noises.

He grimaced. "That's her pack. They've found her. We got out of there just in time."

But then he didn't drive very far, at least I didn't think so, before he stopped the speeder again.

I protested that we should move further along, but he said that we had definitely thrown off the scent, and we were fine. Then he curled up on his side of the speeder, tucking a rolled up blanket under his head and pressing his forehead and antlers into the side of the vehicle, and yawned. He shut his eyes.

So, this was how we were going to sleep?

Sitting up in this speeder?

Of course he'd think that I could sleep that way, but there was no way. I was still very keyed up over everything that had happened, and it was hot in the speeder, and it was not the least bit comfortable.

I was going to be awake all night.

He, on the other hand, seemed to drift off right away. His whole body relaxed and his breathing went even and his face looked relaxed and young and innocent over there, and I hated him.

I made lots of noise trying to dig out something to use as a pillow. I was gratified when he woke up enough to grunt and open his eyes in slits. But he looked at me tucking the other folded up blanket under my head, mimicking the way he'd curled up on my side of the speeder, and he shut his eyes again.

I shut my eyes too, thinking that I would never be able to sleep, never.

But when I woke up, some time had passed. It was just hard to say how long, because it was still dark out—constantly dark. I sat up.

I really, really had to pee.

He was still asleep. His mouth was open and his legs were open, and the, um, the arousal protuberance had come out, but it was just lying there against his leg, soft and small.

I cocked my head at it, but I really couldn't be too interested in it, because of the frantic call of nature I was experiencing here.

I was going to have to deal with this.

I sat up and stretched. I tried to have a talk with my bladder that maybe it could hold off a bit?

Nope, wasn't having it. Needed draining.

I glanced at him. How did *he* pee? If his penis was tucked up inside his body like what I'd read on my bracelet and it wasn't going to come out unless he was riding his mating instinct, then that seemed like a problem for the endocrine system. Maybe that thing there, the protuberance, maybe it was responsible for urination. It did seem to have a little vein up the middle of it, and maybe there was a slit—

Okay, gross.

I didn't need to think about this.

I opened the door to the speeder and climbed down out of it.

Once on the ground, I debated. Should I pee here? What if that was, like, scenting too close to our speeder? What if that would bring that vvoln pack to us?

On the other hand, I didn't want to go too far off on my own into the woods.

I settled for on the other side of a large tree. I relieved myself as quickly as possible and then headed back for the speeder.

In the distance, I heard the wailing of the vvoln pack, and it sent shivers up my spine. My whole body was alight with that.

I wanted to run, but it seemed to make me freeze.

I stopped, looking around, searching high and low for any sign of danger. All I could see was darkness, foliage colored silvery in the light of the stars, shadows of leaves and trees and black emptiness pooling everywhere—so many places that something furry and clawed could be hiding, ready to spring out.

My heart beat fast.

I shot forward, running for the speeder.

Movement.

There. Out of the corner of my eye.

I didn't stop to see what it was. I ran faster. I reached the ladder and hauled myself up.

Then I glanced down, and I saw a pair of antlers rushing through the foliage beneath me.

"Holston?" I called.

The antlers lifted, and a face appeared. It was not Holston. It was another man down there. He looked up at me with widening eyes and then he sniffed the air, jerked his head in another direction, and took off again.

I hurried up the rest of the ladder and yanked the door open.

Holston woke at once, sitting up straight. "Cypra," he said in a sleep-ravaged voice.

"There's someone down there," I said.

He leaned forward. "Vvoln found us?"

"No, another donen," I said. "I saw a donen man with antlers."

Holston furrowed his brow. "No one comes up here during Star Season. Barely anyone comes up here at all, actually."

"I *saw* him."

Holston opened the door and swung down onto the ladder. He climbed down.

I poked my head out and peered after him. I pointed. "He was over there."

Holston went to investigate. "Nothing here now," he said. "But there is a scent." His nostrils flared and his back stiffened.

Suddenly, Holston turned and ran for the ladder to the speeder. He climbed up it quickly, so fast he was practically a blur.

He hurled himself into the speeder with me and he crawled over the seat for me.

I flattened myself against the side of the speeder. "Holston?" I whispered.

"You should probably get out," he said in a strained voice.

"Get out?" I said. "Go back down there?"

"He scented like... competition."

"Competition for what?"

"For your cunt," he growled.

This went through me in a ripple of something horrifying and yet pleasant, and I let out a noisy breath.

"Get away from me," Holston said, still growling.

I turned, trying the door to the speeder.

Holston seized me by the hips and yanked me back against his body.

I… I meant to open the speeder door. I think I meant to.

His fingers wormed over my clothes, no finesse, squeezing me, digging in his fingers, but he somehow got the eazclasp of my pants to release and he yanked them down, exposing my bare ass to him.

I gasped.

He grunted.

His hands were big. They spanned both sides of my hips, his thumbs digging into the swell of my ass, his fingers pressing into my thighs. He rearranged me, pulling my ass back to settle against his crotch and his, um, his protuberance wormed between my legs.

I let out a high pitched noise.

"Fuck," he managed in a mangled voice.

His protuberance was flattening against my labia again, parting them, and it was moving, undulating, little movements going through it like waves over the surface of water.

I moaned. "Good," I said.

"Yeah," he said. "You're so warm and wet and—" He went still, digging his fingers further into me. "No, fuck, no, I am *not* going to—"

I cut him off with another moan. His body had latched onto my clit, molding its way around me there and now the little waves were concentrated there, starting at the edges and traveling inward, right to my center, in a perfect, wondrous pattern that felt like sheer bliss.

He panted. "I can stop," he told me, his voice

strangled. "Give me a hisec. I swear, I can stop."

"Don't stop," I groaned. "Please, please, never stop. Do this forever." It, uh, it felt *really* good. I never felt anything like that before, not even with a toy or something.

His face collided with my back. He nuzzled me there, wheezing, hot breath from his nose on my spine, through my shirt. His lips found me there. He licked my spine.

I sighed. I undulated my hips—tried to—couldn't—he was holding me in place while that lovely wondrous protuberance between his legs worked me in sweet, perfect surges.

His teeth scraped me, and then he had my flesh between his teeth, the place where my shoulder met my neck, the skin there. He wasn't biting hard, not hurting me, just sort of holding me in place.

I shuddered.

My core clenched—not an orgasm, but getting there, an indication I was eager and ready to come for him, to come right on him there, right against him while he held me in place and wouldn't let me move, while he played me like I was a musical instrument.

He growled again, a rumbling that seemed to vibrate through me in a primal way.

I gasped.

My hips moved again, an involuntary movement.

He dug his fingers more deeply into my skin. "Stay still," he ordered into the skin at my neck.

"I..." I was losing it. "I can't help it. *Please.*"

"When you struggle, it makes my pleasure cock—it makes me—it's hard to *think.*"

Pleasure cock, huh? That's what he called it? "Your pleasure cock is what's caressing my clit?" I gasped.

He just groaned his assent, teeth back in my neck, worrying me there.

"Does it feel good for you?" I whispered. "Can your pleasure cock come?"

He jerked against me, his hands moving from my hips. Now, they were banded around my waist. His pleasure cock slid over my pussy, three sweet, slippery strokes, rubbing my labia, rubbing my clit, rubbing me *everywhere*. His teeth dug into my skin at the same time. The effect was bursting pleasure in my core and bright pain at my neck, and they swirled together into something intense and confusing and exciting.

His pleasure cock rippled again, right into my clit, and I felt my pleasure suddenly gather up, like beads of oil all coming together, and I crested in a blinding sweetness.

Only to burst, as if the beads of oil scattered yet again, raining down in wave after wave of pleasure as my orgasm went through me.

His teeth released and he licked me there, frantic. "Shei," he moaned. "Shei, shei, are you…?"

"Yes," I managed. "Yes, yes, *yes*."

And I felt a shudder go through him, answering movement against me, his pleasure cock seeming to send off little jolts that radiated out—like the things that had been teasing me, but less measured, jerkier, more intense.

So, it *could* come.

And, hmm, I liked this, this pleasure cock he had, that was so perfect at wringing pleasure from me, that had orgasms that were like my own. I liked it a lot. Maybe donen men were just a step up from every other species I'd ever fucked before.

I giggled, turning my head, my mouth seeking his.

His lips found mine and we kissed—a long, wet, frantic joining of our tongues while he held me close against him and the bottom halves of our bodies stopped twitching.

Then he released me and the weight of him settled against me, and I got pressed into the speeder seat, which wasn't comfortable, because it bent the other way, and I made a noise of protest, and he rolled off of me.

But this meant that his pleasure cock came off, and I made a little mew of disappointment when it slid away. I thought it might be sort of perfect to fall asleep with it on me, like we could spoon, and it could cup me from behind, just gently caress my pussy?

I slid down to the floor of the speeder and lay my cheek against the seat and moaned.

He breathed.

I moaned again.

Otherwise, there was nothing.

We didn't talk.

The silence stretched on and on, and now it was starting to get really awkward. We were going to have to talk again. We were going to have to look at each other, but I didn't want to lift my head. I wanted to stay just like this, cheek on the seat, legs jelly, facing away from him, for the rest of eternity.

So, I determined I would.

Except the hidosec I decided that, I got uncomfortable. My legs weren't going to be happy this way, tangled up on the floor, and my neck was at an angle that I couldn't sustain and... wow, what had his teeth done to my skin? There had been that moment of pain? Was I bleeding?

I put my hand to my neck and sat up and then

looked at my fingers.

No blood.

"I'm really sorry." His voice was raw.

I looked up at him.

He was looking back at me. He was sitting up, and his pleasure cock was still huge and engorged and it looked sort of slick and gleaming—oh, was that from *me?*

Okay, this was embarrassing.

"It's all right," I said in a very funny voice that didn't even sound like mine.

"It's not." He shook his head. "It's really not all right at all."

"I'm fine," I said, trying to smile.

"Your, um, your shoulder? Are you…? Did I…?"

I twisted to try to look at it, but I couldn't see anything. I touched it. It was tender there, but I couldn't… I didn't feel indentations of his teeth or anything.

"I don't even know what that was," he said softly. "I never did anything like that before. It was like, I don't know, I needed to hold you in place, I needed to… *subdue* you." He made a face and looked away and a tremor of what seemed to be revulsion went through him.

"It's fine," I said again, and now I sounded chirpy. "It's really…" I tried to sit up and realized my pants were tangled around my calves. I couldn't stand upright in the speeder, so I bent over and pulled my pants up. "Fine." I fastened the eazclasp and sat down. "I mean, you didn't damage me. It felt really good. And you said you could stop and I totally told you not to. So, it's, you know, it's my own fault."

He scoffed. He wasn't looking at me.

I fingered my shoulder.

He turned back around and examined it. "You're going to bruise."

I wriggled away from him.

"I seem to like that, marking you, that seems to be making all kinds of weird things happen in there." He glanced down at his crotch. He reached down behind his pleasure cock and felt around, making a face.

"Is it descending?" I breathed.

"I don't know," he said.

"That's how it works, right? This is, um, what was it called, the first mounting?"

He did that shudder of revulsion again.

"So, then your actual cock—do you call it an actual cock—"

"Mating cock."

"Right, your mating cock would descend and you could… could breed then. Could breed *me*. It'll mean you can…"

"You said you had an implant, though, right? You're not fertile. Of course, your scent, I don't get that."

"Really?" I said, sitting up straight. "What? Do I smell fertile?"

"Why do you think this is happening?" He seemed annoyed.

"I'm not," I said. I held up my arm. "See? Implant, right there. It's good for gecycles. You put it in and it's fine."

"And it's a hundred percent effective at always stopping every single one of your cycles?"

"Well… I mean…" I pulled up my bracelet, but when I tried to search for anything, it just said, *Out of range of information networks.*

"Let's go back," he said. "Let me take you back

now."

"No," I said. "I have to get to that ship. It's my mission. It's important."

"Everyone on that ship is dead. It can't be that important."

"I have to get to the ship, whatever it takes, whatever I have to do. There are things on the ship that the resistance needs."

"Okay, but they'll keep, right? Just... if you could give me enough time to go back down there and get my suppressant working again, maybe get your implant looked at? It might be a fogemoon, maybe two—"

"We're already halfway there," I said. "We can get there tomorrow, right?"

He didn't answer me.

"Right?" I said.

"Today," he said. "If we're going, we should go now. I can't sleep any longer."

"Great, let's go," I said. "The sooner we get this done, the less likely that there's any second mounting."

His face twisted. He looked terrified.

"Have you ever..."

"No, it's never descended," he said. "Never once. And whatever I just did with you... it's not *like* that, not usually. I was out of control."

"I liked it," I said in a tiny voice.

"But the second mounting wouldn't be like that. Because the pleasure cock, it can't... I mean, if we somehow managed it face to face, I guess, it could stimulate you, but typically, the mounting, it's less... as far as nature is concerned, the female orgasm is just for ovulation, so the female doesn't need to feel pleasure during the mating, so it's just... I think it might be... brutal." He swallowed. "I don't want to do it. I don't want to ever..."

"Oh, come on," I said, squaring my shoulders. "You're being silly. No one in my own species has clit stimulators attached to their dicks, and we fuck those men all the time anyway, and it's not brutal. Furthermore, I assume sometimes, your species does go off suppressants to reproduce, right?"

"You want this?" He glared at me. "That's what this has been all along. You're on some... what? I guess it's true what they say about human girls, that you're sex addicts who are insatiable and who just want to be shoved full of as many different species' cocks as you can manage, maybe in succession, maybe at the same time, maybe in all of your orif—"

"No."

Silence.

"Sorry." His voice was hoarse.

"No, this isn't actually some weird porn holovid," I said.

"For the record, I don't want this," he said. "I don't want any of this. I just want to go home." He sounded scared and small and lost, and it should have made me feel sympathy, but instead it made me feel annoyed with him, disgusted with his weakness.

"Grow a pair," I said. "Let's stop talking and get this speeder going."

"What?" he said. He repeated the words. "Grow a pair?"

I had said it in English, which was a human language, and he didn't know it. I didn't know English either. My parents hadn't even spoken it. But phrases, sometimes they were passed down, and they wormed their way into my speech.

"It's, uh, it's a human thing. It means... so, I guess

like, humans think that bravery is contained in the testicles?"

"What?" He gave me a confused look.

"Well, not literally. Just a figurative thing, like, grow some balls, it means..." I shook my head. "Never mind."

He furrowed his brow, sitting up. He looked down at his pleasure cock and started to touch it. Then he leaned over the seat and began rummaging through one of his packs. "That would mean that women aren't brave?"

"I... I guess."

"Women are so much braver than men, though." He snorted.

"I mean..."

"They get attacked for sex, and they carry children, and then they give birth, and added to all of that, in both of our species, they're smaller and have less upper body strength than men, so whenever something scary happens, it's objectively scarier for women, so *they* are braver and—"

"It's just a stupid saying."

He came back with a towel and wiped his pleasure cock clean.

I winced. "Sorry for getting you all..."

"What? No, don't be *sorry,* it's just... the *scent,* it's kind of..." He tucked himself back into his fur. "You still want to go to the ship?"

"Obviously."

"And if it happens? If I rape you?"

I shook my head.

"If it *is* brutal?"

"Maybe I do want it," I muttered. "Okay?"

"You want me to force you? To hurt you?"

"Maybe!"

He let out a noise of disbelief.

"You could have stopped just now," I said.

"I..."

"You could have," I insisted. "I'm sure of it. If I really need you to stop, you'll stop."

"We really don't know that," he said. "I've never done this before. I've never *felt* like this before. I should insist that I won't take you anywhere. I should turn the speeder around, no matter what you want."

"Well, why don't you?"

"I *should*." He started the speeder.

"Is that what you're doing?" I said, sitting up straight. "Where are we going?"

"You are fucking me up, shei. Fucking me up *so* bad."

"Holston—"

"We'll be at your ship in a few hihors."

I let out a sigh of relief.

SIX

holston

All right, so sex with women?

I mean, I'd done it.

I hadn't had a number of partners. Five total, three of which were just random flings, back when I was young, when I kept trying it out just to see if I could figure out whatever it was I was supposed to be missing about it all, and I never really could and gave up on it.

Two of them were girlfriends, longterm things.

My longest girlfriend and I had been together for about four gecycles. She left me because she didn't like that I would go off out in the woods and leave her alone for fogemoons at a time. She got lonely. She got so lonely she found her way into other guys' beds. More than one.

At the time, I blamed her.

It's easy to be really self-righteous about that kind of thing, and everyone's always on your side when you were the one that was faithful, and she was the one that cheated.

But then… I don't know, time passed, and I thought more and more about it, and I felt more and more like it wasn't *all* her fault. She should have made different decisions. She should have left me earlier. But I shouldn't have abandoned her like I did.

What was she supposed to do with a relationship with a man who was gone half the time? How was she supposed to feel about being left alone?

I didn't prioritize her, that was the thing.

This.

The outdoors.

Hunting.

Being in the woods alone.

It's always been my most important thing. Nothing is as good as this. Nothing.

And if I was honest with myself, it was partly because sex with women was… I mean, it was good, right, but it was never… I could take it or leave it. It often seemed like a lot of effort to me for not so much payoff.

My girlfriend, she wanted more intimacy, too. She said it wasn't about sex necessarily, but that she liked us having sex, liked the pleasure of it, but what she really liked was us close and connected.

I think… and she never said this, but I think what she liked was that when we were fucking, she was the only thing I was focused on, and I can't say I felt like that most of the time.

She…

I loved her, but I thought of her as a sort of accent to my life. Like, not the meat of life, but the side dish. I could survive without a girlfriend, right? I could survive without sex. It was nice to have, but when it demanded sacrifices from me? Well, the sacrifices weren't worth it, so I didn't make them.

And that's why she cheated on me.

Because she could tell that she didn't matter enough to me.

I didn't know why I was thinking about this while I was driving this speeder up to Cypra's ship. I had a feeling that she and I were kind of the same in this way, though. Like, Cypra needed to get to that ship. The resistance was really important to her.

She'd made sacrifices for the resistance, see? It mattered to her.

Similarly, while I never made sacrifices for my girlfriend, I definitely made sacrifices to be out here hunting.

It was all a give and take, right?

Being out here, living in the wild, it wasn't easy. It wasn't comfortable. A guy didn't come out hunting animals because it was simple. The difficulty was part of it. You sacrificed comfort for the payoff of the accomplishment. The accomplishment meant more *because* of the sacrifice.

So, I knew when Cypra said things to me like she wanted me to force myself on her, it wasn't really about wanting me. It was about the sacrifice. Getting to that ship *meant* more if she sacrificed everything, including her body, to get there.

I just didn't want to be that thing she was sacrificing herself to.

No.

That was a lie.

I wanted…

Fuck, I had never wanted anything like the way I wanted her.

Right now, if you had said to me, "Choose. Cypra's pussy or hunting." No question. I wanted to fuck her. I wanted to fuck her now. I wanted to put my pleasure cock on her again and again and again, and I wanted whatever was stirring inside my pelvis, straining and trying to work its way out of me? That. I wanted to put *that* in her.

So, the thing was, this was just all very fucked up.

Because I knew she didn't really want me, but I was trying to make it her fault somehow, like make it that I was doing her a favor, when I was really taking advantage of her martyrdom to use her body for my pleasure.

It was disgusting.

I didn't think I was this sort of man.

I hated myself.

And it didn't matter, because the mating urge inside me was too strong. The mating urge was making me into some kind of monster, and I was paying lip service to the idea that I was fighting it, but I had surrendered a long time ago.

I drove the speeder and we went further and further north, heading toward the coordinates of her ship. We couldn't lock on to the coordinates, because there were no signals and no network up here. But the speeder had internal maps, downloaded when we were in range of the networks, and I could follow those to get there.

We traveled in silence, but I could smell her, and my body was, uh, was changing. I could feel it, things inside me waking up and rearranging. There was an uncomfortable pressure in my pelvis—but the discomfort was also pleasurable, a promise of something to come.

From what I understood, after a first mounting, my mating cock could descend as soon as the span of a day-night cycle (about eight hihors). It might take longer. I didn't know if it would take longer because it was the first time it had ever descended. But I was excited by it, and I felt vaguely miffed at myself for never *wanting* this to happen.

My body was designed to do this, so why had I never wanted to take it out for a test run?

At any rate, I was enjoying the fact I was experiencing it, and I was thinking all sorts of filthy thoughts about Cypra.

I *liked* her human body.

Her little hairless ass cheeks, all rounded and smooth? Digging my fingers into her while I pressed between her soft, smooth thighs? It was enough to make my eyes roll back in my head at the thought of it.

I considered doing it again.

My pleasure cock had no objections to the idea of it.

I could stop driving, jump her, and she'd… what? Would she fight me? I thought I could do it anyway, even if she did.

That was *gross*.

I had *not* just thought that.

I tightened my jaw, stared out the window of the speeder, and resolved not to touch her. Those thoughts were just my instinct. This was why we had suppressants, because this was what our mating was like.

The way I understood it, the way it used to be, my ancestors would come up here and it would be a free-for-all. Women would separate from the men and go running off to hide. And men would chase them. I didn't know if the chasing was part of it, like some kind of game, or if… if maybe the women didn't *want* to be bred cycle after cycle, having litters of two to four children after every Star Season, nursing them, weaning them, only to be forced to leave the young with the older generation once Star Season came around again. To be forced to go back up to the pole again and it all to start *over*.

And maybe the men didn't want to do it either. It was difficult for them as well. They often bulked up before the season, overeating because it would be a stretch of time in which they had no time to feed themselves, only to fight off predators, fight off competitors, and breed, breed, breed. Lots of men didn't survive the season amongst my ancestors. Lots of women didn't survive either, of course.

It had been brutal.

Just...

But it was instinct. My body was forcing me to do this for the survival of my species. We'd evolved this way to counter-balance our high mortality rates, so to my mating instinct, little things like whether I consented or she consented didn't matter. To my mating instinct, when she struggled, I liked it more, because liking struggling ensured that I didn't stop for struggling, that I bred her no matter *what*.

Gross.

I was out of control.

But I was capable of noticing that, commenting on it, thinking about it.

And yet, still, somehow incapable of stopping.

Maybe that's not true, said an oily voice at the back of my brain. *Maybe you could stop. Maybe it's only that this is what you really are, something selfish and driven by pleasure.*

When Gillifa—my girlfriend, the one who cheated on me—asked me to sacrifice for her, asked me to make her my priority, who did I pick?

Did I pick her?

No. I picked hunting. I picked me.

And now, this woman… I could protect her.

Instead, I was going to make use of her.

Fuck, I was a piece of shit.

Turn the speeder around, I urged myself.

I hit the brakes.

Cypra jerked next to me, gripping the handrest on the side of the speeder. "What's going on?"

"I've changed my mind," I said. "I'm not doing this. We're going back. I'm better than this."

She reached across the speeder and put her hand on my chest. "No. Wait."

"Look, I get that you're willing to do whatever it takes to get to that ship, but you're not turning me into a rapist—or it's my fault. I'm turning *myself* into—I'm not doing it."

"It's not going to be rape. Stars!" She pressed into me and put her mouth on mine.

I jerked back.

She jerked back too, looking chagrined. "Okay, fine. Fine, then. You're, it's all instinct to you, and you probably think I'm some gross human slut or whatever from the way you talk about me. You resent that your body is making you attracted to me against your will. Sorry. My attraction is genuine. Yours isn't."

My jaw worked. I furrowed my brow. "Wait. What?"

"I'm not saying any of that again." She hurled herself across the speeder, shaking her head. She looked out the window. "Fine. Let's go back, then. This is mortifying. It's probably… it's the other way around, I guess. I'm taking advantage of your mating instinct to coerce you. It's against *your* will. *I'm* the rapist."

"No, that's an insane thing to say," I said.

"Well, look, whatever it is," she said, "it's a bad situation for us to be in, and… I don't want it like this, not really." She slumped down in the seat. "What you said before, about how we take a little time to look at my implant, make sure it's working, and to get your suppressant working again, it makes sense. I think I protested so much just because I've had some weird fixation with you since the hisec you said that thing to me about how my pussy was wet and you could smell it."

"That was disgusting that I said that," I said. "That was... that was the first clue that something was *wrong* with me."

"I know," she said. "Believe me, I know. I'm not exactly proud of being turned on by that. I think... the truth is, I've just let it go too long. Sex is a basic need for all people, and I've been neglecting myself, and now I'm having this utterly inappropriate reaction to you, and it'll be better if we..." She groaned. "Oh, stars, just turn *around*. I'm going to stop *talking*." She put both of her hands over her face.

"Hey," I said, my voice going gentle. "You don't have to be embarrassed. This is all me."

She shook her head, keeping her hands over her face.

I backed the speeder up. I pulled it forward, but there wasn't enough room on the road here to pull around, so I had to back up again.

Bang.

The speeder rocked.

Cypra tore her hands away from her face. "What was that?"

I tried to urge the speeder forward. But it wasn't going to happen, because the back corner of the speeder was tilted downwards. "Blowout," I said.

"What?"

"We've got a flat tire." I turned off the speeder and

thrust open the door. I climbed down the ladder to the ground.

"You have a spare, right?" she called down after me, her head poking out from my side of the speeder.

"I have a patch kit," I called back. "These tires, they're huge. Lugging around a spare, it's not feasible."

"O-okay," she said.

What I didn't say was that I was pretty sure the patch kit was going to be worthless. Because a loud sound like that, it probably meant that the tire was shredded.

I went around to the back of the vehicle to inspect.

Oh, yeah. I could already see that pieces of the tire were scattered around on the ground. This was bad. It was probably my fault. I hadn't checked the speeder out before we took off, not thoroughly. I'd been distracted. This tire probably had some damage on it already, maybe a place that was weakened and then what happened was that when the tire was in use, the air pressure moved around and kept stretching that weak spot until… boom.

Now, if I was out here by myself, it wouldn't be that big of a deal. I'd note where I left the vehicle and go back on foot. I'd have someone come out here and pick it up—probably after the Star Season was over so I could have a hover speeder come out here. Sun would be necessary to power the hover speeders, so it'd be a while. It would be inconvenient not having this speeder, but I'd manage.

With Cypra here, however, it was just bad.

"Holston?" came her voice. "You can fix it, right?"

I rubbed at my antlers and stared at the ruined tire, and I didn't answer her.

"Holston?"

"I, uh, I fucked up, shei," I called back to her.

"What do you mean?" It was her shrill voice again.

I sighed.

She was climbing down the ladder now. She alighted on the ground and came around to take in the tire and the pieces of exploded tire and her lips parted and she let out a little breathy noise of dismay. "You can't patch that."

"Not so much."

"So... so... we don't have a speeder?" Now, her voice was very shrill.

"I should have looked over the tires. I should have checked the pressure. I should have given the vehicle a better once over before we left. It's on me. If I'd looked, I would have seen this."

"Okay, but who *cares?*"

"Well, it's my—"

"It's the past. What do we do *now?*"

I blew out a breath and worried at the tip of one of my antlers with my thumb. "Uh, well, this ship of yours, what kind of shape is it in?"

"I don't know. No one knows. It broadcasted coordinates and then it went dark."

"It's probably better shelter for you than the woods, though," I said. "It'd take us gesuns to get back to any kind of civilization, and if I'm, um, in a rut, you'll be running from me as much as from the vvoln, and, uh, at least in the ship, you could probably hunker down?"

"Is there any way we can call for help?"

I shook my head. "No signal out here, shei."

"Why do you keep *calling* me that?"

"I just call women that," I muttered.

"Have you considered that it's sexist and reductive and disgusting?" She gestured with both hands.

I shifted on my hooves, clearing my throat. "Uh, sorry, Cypra."

She turned away from me. "No, it's… this isn't your fault. I did this to myself."

"No, no, you didn't. It is my fault. I didn't check the tires—"

"I should probably stop yelling at you if I don't want to bring down all the vvoln on us, including the pack that we pissed off already, huh?" Her voice trembled.

I sighed again. "Look, we'll probably only have to sleep outside once and then we'll be able to make it to the ship. We'll have a fire, and we'll be safe from the vvoln. And my, uh, my mating cock should stay inside me for that long, I think."

"That's not what I read," she said. "It could be really soon. It could already be—"

"It's not." I gestured to my crotch with both hands. "See? It's not."

She bit down on her bottom lip. "So, um, when you said… said 'brutal,' um, you have any specifics there?"

I couldn't look at her.

When I did, her eyes were filling with tears again, and I felt like my heart was getting ripped from my chest, and I went to her. I started to touch her, to comfort her, and then I thought better of it.

I didn't touch her. My voice was rough. "I will do everything in my power to keep myself from… from any of it."

"But you can't control it," she said, her voice wavering.

"No, I can," I said. "I'll find a way."

She looked away, surreptitiously wiping at her eye.

"Hey," I whispered. "I promise you."

SEVEN

cypra

It was strange how all over the place my emotions were about this.

One hisec, I was positive I could handle Holston's mating cock, mounting me, all of it. I needed to do it for the resistance, so I'd do it, no problem.

Stars, I was even turned on by it.

I had read all the theories about women and why some of them have rape fantasies. And, okay, I was a woman who had occasionally had rape fantasies. I guessed there wasn't any point in denying it.

There was one theory that women did it because they had been brought up in a culture that taught them to deny their sexual urges and said they were shameful. I knew there were cultures like that out there, but my upbringing as a human woman on the Colony, sex was just *part* of being a human woman. So, I'd never felt shamed for wanting sex, not really.

That just didn't really ring true to me, but I supposed it might for some women's fantasies. This way, they could indulge themselves but it wasn't their fault. The man took utter responsibility for all of the desire, and she could pretend she didn't have any desires at all.

The other theory I'd read was that rape fantasies were about being irresistible. Being so sexy that a man couldn't control himself and *had* to have you. Which… yeah, rang truer for me, definitely.

Which was probably why I'd found this entire situation arousing at all, what with Holston being out-of-control into me in that way. It was like a fantasy come to life.

Except I was beginning to realize that maybe fantasies should *stay* fantasies.

Because this was starting to not seem arousing at all, just scary.

So, here I was, one hisec ready and willing and the next timid and frightened.

I felt bad for Holston vowing to me that he was somehow going to fight his instincts, because I could see how difficult that was going to be for him, and besides, he shouldn't even be out here. I had gotten us into this situation by insisting we come out here at all, by not agreeing with him when he said we should turn back.

Maybe this was what I deserved.

Maybe I was just asking for it.

Oh, stars, was I victim-blaming myself?

But weren't we both victims in this case? Victims of his instinct, his biology, the plant pollen in this region of the planet, the vvoln themselves, the busted tire?

I didn't blame him.

But maybe I was just saying that to myself because I also needed him. If he left me alone in the wilderness out here, I would die. Either I'd get lost and starve or I'd be eaten by vvoln or…

Well, I did need him.

And if that meant that I had to let him, uh, mount me, well…

I wanted to ask him a thousand questions. Was he

going to go totally mad? Would he be able to talk? Would he be a mindless fuck machine? How was this going to go down?

But I got the impression he had no idea.

This had never happened to him.

He was terrified too. He was just as scared as I was, if not more.

We pushed the speeder off the road and got all of our supplies out of it. We strapped packs onto our backs and we hiked off into the starry woods.

He went first, his bow slung over his arm, his hooves picking out a sure path between the trees. We didn't stay on the road because it wasn't the quickest way to the coordinates of the ship, so we took a straighter path towards it, going through the trees and underbrush.

I asked how the leaves grew when there was no sun.

He said they didn't, that by the end of Star Season, they'd be on the ground, browned and dead, and all the trees would be bare limbs.

This was just the beginning of Star Season, then.

So, there was no reprieve for us, nothing from the planet itself.

It would be gemoons before the sun returned to the pole.

We didn't talk much. I wanted to. I wanted to ask questions. I wanted to apologize. I wanted to try to explain why I would say things that were so contradictory—that I was genuinely attracted to him one hisec and then start crying at the thought of sex with him.

Maybe I wanted to talk about it, because I thought if I did talk, it would make more sense to me.

But we just walked.

We ate ration bars for the lunchtime meal, and then

kept going for hihors.

Eventually, I lost all desire to talk because I was exhausted. I wanted to stop. I was not used to walking this long. The pack on my back had been totally bearable at the beginning. Now, it felt like I was lugging a trinx on my back. My legs hurt. My neck hurt from the pack pulling on my shoulders. The place where he'd used his teeth on me? Yeah, that didn't feel good either. My back hurt. My muscles were sore from all the movement.

I wanted to collapse.

When he finally called for a halt, I fell into a heap on the ground, and I didn't move. I offered to help make the fire, but I didn't move to do anything, and he didn't give me any orders.

He gathered branches and fed them to the blaze. Then he disappeared and came back quickly with something dead. It was some kind of small furry thing. I watched while he cut up its belly and ripped off its skin, while he pulled out its guts and tossed them on the fire to hiss and pop.

It was disgusting, obviously, the dead animal, but it was mesmerizing too, how skilled he was with it, how quick and efficient.

Once it was spitted and roasting over the fire, the smell was positively mouthwatering and oddly soporific.

I fell asleep and had to be woken up to eat.

"Oh, stars," I muttered around a mouthful, wiping off the grease that was running down my chin. "I've never tasted anything this good."

He laughed. "Yeah, there's nothing like a meal after a long day of walking, that's for sure."

"It's like… it's better out here," I breathed, looking

up at the sky. "Like it means more somehow?"

"Exactly," he said, giving me a grin. He was crouched on the ground, resting his forearms on his knees, hooves on display, and I had a full-on view of his crotch and there was no… but I looked away before he could tell I was checking him for his descended penis and scrotum. "You, uh, the resistance, it's pretty important to you?"

"Obviously," I said. "I mean, someone has to do something about the Toth."

He shrugged.

"Don't you agree? Don't tell me you *like* the Toth."

He shrugged again. "The way I figure it, if it's not the Toth, it'll be someone else. There's always got to be someone in charge like that, and whoever it is, whoever *likes* being in charge, it's usually because they find it gratifying. It's selfish."

I furrowed my brow, thinking about that. "Well, maybe, but that doesn't mean it can't be better, because it can."

He shrugged again.

"You don't think so?"

"I…" He looked into the fire. "I mean, things change, and maybe they get better for someone when they do. But I feel like it's a balance. When something gets better for one group of people, it means it gets worse for someone else."

"So, what? It's pointless? We should give up?"

"I'm not saying that. Things don't have to have a point." He bit into his meat.

"Yes, they do."

He chewed. "Sometimes the point is just that it's gratifying is all, I guess. The best thing you can do is to try to make sure the thing that gives you pleasure hurts the least amount of other people, I guess."

"That seems really..." I cut myself off.

"What?"

"No, never mind. It's fine. You should do whatever you want, actually."

"What were you going to say?"

"I don't want to piss you off. I want you to keep feeding me."

He laughed. "Now, you gotta tell me, shei."

I thought about pointing out he was calling me that again, but if my last outburst about it hadn't stopped him, nothing was going to. I ate another bite of meat, using my teeth to get it off the bone, licking my fingers. It really was good. "I guess it just sounds kind of shallow and empty and meaningless."

"Okay." He was laughing again. "Tell me how you really feel."

"You made me tell you." I gestured with the bone at him.

He was smiling at me. "Why is your resistance thing so meaningful, then?"

"Because it helps other people."

"Does it?"

"Yes."

"You sure it's really about other people, though? I mean, you don't get a charge out of having important missions, things that are difficult and dangerous? That doesn't make you feel like you're special?"

"Shut up," I said. "You don't have to be like this just because I said you were being—"

"I'm just saying, it *is* gratifying," he said. "And, you know, whatever. I could tell myself that this hunting thing I do out there, that I'm doing good for donenkind at large, because wild-hunted meat is healthier and better for the planetary environment and more ethical than keeping animals penned up in farms and all kinds of crap. If I wanted to believe what I did was good for people, I could spin myself a story."

"Look, the resistance *is* doing good. It's not a spin—"

"Sure," he said. "It is. And you wouldn't be able to keep doing that good for the galaxy if it didn't make you feel special."

I shook my head at him. "You're interpreting it all weird."

"Here's a question for you." He raised a finger. "You have any brothers or sisters?"

"No," I said.

"What about your parents?"

"What about *your* parents?"

"Dad's gone, but I see my mother probably two or three times a gemoon," he said. "What if your mom got real sick and needed you to quit the resistance and come home to take care of her?"

I scoffed.

"You're just a selfless, sweet receptacle of good for the galaxy," he said in a mocking tone. "So—"

"Okay, you made your point," I muttered. "I do like it."

"It matters to you," he said. "You wouldn't give it up for anything."

"I wouldn't give it up," I said. "It matters. Not just to me... but I guess, yeah, fine, to me, too. It's, like, sort of part of my identity."

"I totally get that," he said, grinning at me. "I really do."

I sighed, shaking my head. He didn't get it.

"Don't feel ashamed of that," he said. "Or... I don't know, sometimes *I* feel ashamed of it, I guess. I want to be…"

"Be what?"

"I wonder what it would feel like if there was someone else, someone more important than all that, someone I'd put first, above everything."

I thought about that. Was there someone *I'd* put ahead of the resistance?

Sienne, my contact, my friend, she was devoted to the resistance, but I knew that her priority was always to Caspe, who was her husband and partner, and that he came first.

What if I had someone like that?

"You, uh, I guess you don't date much?" I said.

"It never works out," he said.

"Because you don't put them first?" I whispered.

He looked back into the fire.

"Why not?" I said.

"You don't seem to date much either, shei." He still wasn't looking at me.

"Well, I don't have much chance to meet men," I said. "When I do, I can't tell them I'm with the resistance."

"You told me."

"Yeah, I don't know why I did that."

He turned away from the fire, then, capturing my gaze with his own, and we stared into each other's eyes for too long. Something wordless passed between us.

I was the one who broke it, looking down to shove the remaining bit of meat I was eating into my mouth. I chewed and swallowed. "If I fell in love with someone, I'm sure I'd put them first. Or maybe, maybe if he was with the resistance too, he'd understand, and he wouldn't ask me to choose."

"I don't think so," said Holston.

"What? Why not?"

"I just think people want to mean something to their partners," he said. "They want to mean everything."

"Maybe," I said. I yawned.

"You tired?"

"I'm not used to that much physical exercise, not like you."

"Well, you sleep, then. I'll set an alarm to wake up and make sure the fire's burning, okay?"

"No, I can help," I said. "If we need to keep watch or we need to—"

"Shei, I can do this. Sleep."

I curled up on the ground. As I did, something occurred to me. "Holston?"

"Hmm?"

"Should we talk about *why* there was another donen man last night?"

"Who knows about that," he said. "Maybe some asshole came up here for a cheap thrill."

"His scent? His scent made you react, so does that mean he's not on suppressants?"

Nothing from Holston.

I sat up.

He was tending the fire. "Guy's a fucking idiot if so."

"But then... if he's out here, and he's not on suppressants, and he..." I swallowed. "Is he coming for me too?"

He glanced at me. "Shit," he muttered.

"Would you have to... fight him?"

His lips parted, and I suddenly smelled him, smelled his rising musk and he smelled good. Did it turn him on to think about fighting someone for me?

It maybe turned me on.

Terrified me, though, but also...

Oh, stars, here I was, waffling back and forth again on this. *Why* was it so confusing?

He turned away, with effort. "Go to sleep," he said in a raw voice.

I lay back down. My heart was pounding. My body felt taut, like the strap of a bow pulled back. My nipples tingled. My pussy pulsed.

Moments passed.

I spoke again, my voice breathy and affected. "Is your, um, did it descend yet?"

"Shei…" His voice was a warning.

"If it's just your… just your pleasure cock…?"

"Lose me in deep space, Cypra, I *promised* you—"

"Do you want to?" I whispered. I sat up again.

He was crouched just a few feet away, gazing at me like I was the only thing he'd ever wanted in his entire life, like I was his *world*.

I reached for him. "I'm sorry if I'm being so hot and cold. I don't mean to confuse you like that. I'm confused too. I don't know what this is."

He groaned. "The more that I get your scent, you know, the more…"

"The more what?"

"I mean, I think it'll make me… I don't really know." He reached out and took my hand, the one I was reaching out to him. He tugged on me.

I scrambled up and went to him.

He settled on the ground, crossing his furry hooved legs, and he pulled me into his lap. He touched my face. "This is wrong," he whispered, his voice a caress. "You just said you were confused."

I leaned into his touch, shutting my eyes. "I am confused, but I don't think it's wrong."

He kissed me.

I moaned against his tongue, wrapping my arms around his neck, turning to press into him.

He dragged his hands over my back, over my waist—sending shivers all through me—and then up to my shoulders. One of his fingers found the place where his teeth had marked me, and he traced his forefinger over the bruised skin as his tongue danced gently with mine.

I moved my leg, straddling him, pressing my crotch against his crotch, my chest against his.

He grunted, breaking our kiss.

I touched his antlers, running my fingers over them.

He shuddered.

"Are they sensitive?" I was delighted.

"No," he said thickly.

I giggled, gently running my fingertips over them.

He shivered again. His nipples tightened and goosebumps broke out all over his ribs.

I giggled. "Beg to differ, Holston."

He seized my wrist and stopped me. He kissed me again, hard.

I moaned, writhing against him.

I felt his pleasure cock responding, worming free and wriggling in against me, snuggling in against the heat that was radiating through my pants. I cried out at the sensation of it.

He sighed, and he put his hands inside my shirt, inside my supporter, cupping my breasts.

I threw my head back.

"Maybe," he whispered, mouth on my throat, "it's only right that I give you pleasure first, especially if I'm going to lose control and take you."

I convulsed against him—affected by the thought of his "taking" me.

His pleasure cock started to make those little surges, like waves. They went over my clit and it felt wondrous. His mouth was on my neck. His fingers teased my nipples. And his pleasure cock worked me through my pants. I was undone.

I let out a series of moans, and he whispered to me, lips and tongue finding my earlobe, "You like that?"

Obviously I liked it. No, I was moaning for no freaking reason.

"Say it, shei, tell me you like it," he growled in my ear.

Mmph, I liked being ordered around like that, actually. "I like it," I gasped.

"What do you like?"

"Your… your hands," I breathed. "Your fingers on my nipples."

"Your hard, *hard* little pretty nipples," he said. "Hard like rocks for me."

"Yes," I gasped.

"And what else do you like?"

"I like your—"

"Shh." He slammed his fingers over my mouth suddenly, and his whole body went still, well, everything except his pleasure cock, which jammed into me in a series of jerky twitches and suddenly tipped me into a half-crest, an almost orgasm.

I groaned against his fingers, unable to stop myself.

"Shei." He was fierce.

What?

Did he hear something?

What was going on?

I forced myself to be still, but my pussy started to twitch, chasing an orgasm like a greedy girl with a mind of her own.

He lifted me and set me down next to him and was on his hooves, prowling out to the edge of the light from the fire.

"What is it?" I whispered.

He held a hand back at me, but gazed out into the darkness. "I heard—"

Suddenly, there was a flash of tusks and claws and Holston went backwards, landing in the fire in a shower of sparks, a vvoln growling into his face.

EIGHT

cypra

I screamed.

I know. Totally girly thing to do.

He was *in* the fire, though.

He rolled out of it, letting out a scream of his own, rolling on top of the vvoln.

The vvoln shied from the sparks that had come up, backing away. It growled at us both, fierce, threatening.

I picked up the knife that he'd used to skin the animal we'd cooked. I brandished it, going for the vvoln.

"Shei!" he screeched.

"What?" I said. "I'm not going to just cower here and be the stupid woman while you fight the big, scary beast."

"Uh, how many of those big, scary beasts have you killed?"

"Well, none, but that doesn't mean I can't kill them."

"Granted, granted," he said. "But we should play to our strengths, huh?"

I stabbed at the vvoln.

It backed up further, letting out another growl.

Holston was next to me. "Give me the knife," he said. "You build up the fire."

"Oh, okay," I said, nodding. "Yeah, I can do that." I

gave him the knife and I turned to the fire.

Build it up, right.

I mean, that meant, uh, what? Adding wood?

Well, Holston had gathered a handy pile over here, so I'd just grab one of these big logs…

Wait, I'd done this before, put on a big log and it had totally smothered the fire. I needed to get some smaller kindling to get it going hot before I tried to get this big log on. I set it down and gathered up handfuls of the smaller twigs that were sitting next to it.

Crouching next to the blaze, I fed it the twigs, letting it get bigger and bigger, and then I went over to get the log and I nudged it in.

It didn't catch right away.

I got more twigs, pushing them in, here and there. Fires were kind of complicated, weren't they?

Oh. There. It was catching.

"Good," said Holston. "That's good. It'll take a while to burn that down."

"Are you going to kill the vvoln?" I said. "I thought you said they were afraid of fire. Why did it do that?"

"Because we were…"

"Oh," I said. "Is it attracted to the smell of sex?"

"I mean, they were the number one natural predator of donen," he said. "And they were attracted to this region because it's where we mate. So… probably?"

"Sorry," I whispered. "It's my fault."

"Hey, you know what? No more of this blame shit. It's both of our faults. It's no one's fault. We're just… we're going to survive. And if I kill it…"

"Its pack will come."

"We're safe here, with the fire," he said. "If we can get it big enough… Safe enough to get some rest."

"We're not sleeping with a vvoln stalking around

our campfire!" I was horrified.

"It's the best option, I think."

"Why?"

"Well, if we kill it and run, then once its pack finds us, it'll track us easy. And we'll be exhausted, because we won't have slept. So, I think we should get some rest." He glanced at his shoulder and winced.

"Oh, stars, you got burned!" I went to him, reaching out to examine his back and shoulders.

"I'm fine." But he let me look at him. His skin was red. There were blisters in a few places.

My fingers hovered over the wounds. "This doesn't look good." But I noticed that the place where he'd been scratched by the vvoln the other day was entirely closed up. It looked a fogemoon old, not a few hihors old.

"I've got an ointment in my pack," he said. "It's crazy expensive. It's this formula that handlers get for gladiators. I'm fine. I'll get it." He went over to his pack.

I sat next to the fire, staring at the vvoln, which was pacing back and forth on the edge of the darkness, growling at us. I shook my head. "You know, most animals that are afraid of fire, don't... don't..."

"Yeah, well, that vvoln is worked up for some reason," he said.

"I can't sleep with that thing there."

"We'll sleep in shifts," he said. "You go first."

"No way, you go first," I said, eyeing the vvoln. "You can go to sleep like *that*." I snapped my fingers. "It takes me a while. I'd rather get more tired."

"Well, if you're sure?"

"I'm not. I want to go on the record that I don't like this." I glanced back at him. "I guess you didn't bring a blaster?"

"I don't really use them," he said. "They destroy perfectly good meat by scorching it."

"Great," I muttered.

"The resistance, they didn't arm you?"

"I didn't want to take guns from them," I muttered. "They need them for really important missions. And this isn't that dangerous. And... anyway, I'm not really great with blasters."

"What's there to be great with? You point a blaster and pull the trigger." He was dismissive. He curled up on the other side of the fire. "Any idiot can kill anything with a blaster. It takes skill to use a bolts and bow."

"Well, when you want things dead, blasters are handy," I snapped.

He scoffed, arranging himself so that he was mostly on his belly, so as not to hurt his shoulder and back. He shut his eyes.

"So, when do I wake you up?" I said.

"Two hihors," he said. "It's not really enough sleep, but it'll have to do."

They were on a schedule on this planet of sleeping for four hihors after being up for eight hihors. If they were really tired, they'd get up for hihors and then sleep again when it was dark. Days here were very short. It seemed to me that they didn't sleep nearly enough, but I'd been sleeping as much as he had now for a while, and I seemed all right.

He yawned.

He was going to be asleep in two hidosecs, wasn't he?

Yeah, sure enough, he was out like a plastorch. I glared at him and then turned back to the vvoln.

It growled at me.

I stifled a whimper.

Go away, I thought at it.

And then it did, backing away into the shadows.

But I found I didn't like that, because I could hear something out there, in the woods, rustling around in the trees and underbrush, and I didn't know what it was. Was it the vvoln, going in circles around our campfire?

I sat with my back to the fire, hugging my knees, and I didn't move.

In the distance, I could hear the wailing of the vvoln. It was a bone-chilling noise that seemed to echo off the starry sky overhead.

I didn't like this place, this place of perpetual night, where the only safety was this small fire.

After a while, I got up to put more logs on it. It probably didn't need it. The fire was plenty hot—and it was not exactly cold up here, considering this planet was hot all the time. Of course, without the heavy atmospheric cover here, it was less humid, a dryer heat, and the trees helped somewhat too, though I couldn't say why, because obviously, there was no shade in the dark.

But feeding the fire and tending it gave me something to do, and I wanted to make sure it didn't go out. I wanted there to be no chance of that.

While I was feeding the fire more twigs and branches, I heard a noise.

I tried to convince myself it was the wailing of vvoln, but it was different.

It sounded like a scream.

It was close.

I stood up, and I heard something thrashing out

there, something in the woods.

"Hello?" I called.

Someone responded, but not in Common. They were speaking Cobran, which was a trading language from the Lanisson sector. I was pretty terrible with it. I could count to ten and I knew my colors, but otherwise, nothing.

A woman appeared, shrieking in Cobran. She was a donen, and she was naked, but I guessed they were always naked. Still, I'd never seen one with breasts like that, huge, swaying naked breasts, and she was dirty and her hair was matted and she pumped her her hooved legs and came for me, tears streaming down her face and then—

The vvoln came from the side and tackled her.

NINE

cypra

I screamed.

The vvoln drove its tusks into her midsection.

She cried out in pain and terror.

I went for the bolts and bow, trying to figure out how to use it.

The vvoln was tearing its tusks into this woman, rooting out her guts, goring her in half.

I was moaning, my hands shaking, lifting the bow.

And Holston was there, taking the weapon from me.

He shot the vvoln, and the bolt went right into its eye, and the vvoln wavered on its feet and collapsed on the woman.

She let out a serious of gasping panicked cries, looking down at her ruined body.

Holston loaded another bolt.

"Holston," I breathed.

He shot the woman in the temple. She went still.

I shoved him. "What the fuck?"

"All that woman was thinking about was pain," Holston said to me softly. "And she was *going* to die."

"But you… you… you don't know that."

"I do."

He turned back to the fire and started kicking at it with his hooves. "We have to go."

"What was that woman doing out here?"

He shook his head. "I have no idea." He furrowed his brow. "But she was... she looked fertile."

"You can see that?"

He glanced down at my breasts.

I folded my arms over them. "Oh, well, I did notice she was..." I knew some species were like that, that their breasts only got swollen for mating or to feed their young. "Fine. So... what? You think people are up here for the mating season?"

"No one does that. People haven't done it in a hundred gecycles," he said. He went out to look down at her body, and to look down at the body of the vvoln. "Maybe her and that guy we saw? Some stupid kinky thing with them."

"If they came out here for fun sexy time, and she's dead, we have to tell him."

"How do you suppose we do that?"

"Well, he was chasing her, right, like, for fun? So, he must be nearby, and we should call for him—"

"And bring the vvoln down on us, you mean? Bring them down faster, because they're going to come to the scent of the blood."

I grimaced.

He went back to the fire. "Help me put this out, shei. We need to *go*."

* * *

holston

I went to examine the dead woman for a bracelet or some way of identifying her, but there was nothing. I noted the coordinates on my bracelet instead, hoping that when we got back, I could notify someone and they could find whatever remained of her for her family. It wouldn't be much, unfortunately, not after the vvoln were done with her. They'd hollow her out, just like with that jurrn we'd come across.

We left the fire as only barely smoking and took off into the woods.

Cypra stayed close to me now, huddling in, her body giving of a mingled scent of fear and fertility that was making my pleasure cock constantly engorged and making things twitch inside me, things that were trying to get out of me. But it was more important now than ever that I keep control of myself.

Because the vvoln were going to come for us.

Maybe they'd be distracted by the remains of that woman back there. Maybe the pack would eat before they tried to follow us. I couldn't be sure.

I got the impression Cypra hadn't really realized what the vvoln did to people. She'd probably never seen a person be attacked like that, ripped apart like that.

The vvoln liked to do that, to rip their prey up, leave them alive while they feasted. I didn't know if it was malice or what. Maybe they liked the flavor of the meat when it was tinged with fear and pain.

I put an arm around her, which was supposed to be reassuring, but which was probably a bad idea. "So, new plan. We push on until we get to the ship, only stopping to eat ration bars and have water."

She looked warily out into the darkness. "There could be vvoln out there, right now, keeping pace with us. They could kill us."

"No way, shei. I won't let anything happen to you."

She nestled into me. "I don't think you can promise that. I saw how fast it was. If it pounced on us from behind—"

"I'd hear it."

She pressed her lips together.

I rubbed her shoulder, tightening my arm around her. "I won't let anything happen to you."

Inside my pelvis, my mating cock tried to lengthen and harden, but it ran into resistance. Ouch.

I grunted, letting go of her, reaching down to try to rearrange myself.

"What's… is it happening?" she breathed.

"No, it's fine," I grunted. My cock *wanted* to come out. I tried to tuck it further away. Okay, that was just going to be uncomfortable. Fine. I could handle discomfort.

"Holston—"

"It's fine," I insisted. "We're getting to the ship."

We walked.

We walked for hihors.

We stopped to eat and drink, and then we got back on hooves and feet and walked some more.

My cock slowly worked itself out, and it was, uh, just hanging there, but it was soft, and I decided I didn't need to say anything to Cypra about it, because it would only freak her out. It was freaking me out. I did my best not to look at her or touch her or smell her, because I didn't know what happened if I did get aroused?

Did it go to my head? Did I lose control?

That couldn't happen.

Not only because I didn't want to hurt her or force her, but because if we were occupied like that, we were vulnerable to vvoln.

There was no sign yet that the vvoln pack of the one I'd killed by the campfire was coming for us, but there was nothing stopping them following our trail.

We could go out of our way to go through the river

again, but that would cost us hihors of time, and I figure it made better sense to get to the ship and get to shelter.

We were close, probably about thirty hidosecs from the ship, when Cypra stopped walking suddenly.

"I can't," she said. "I need a break."

"But we're almost there," I said. "It's less than a hihor at this point. Less than a *half* a hihor. Come on."

She was looking at my crotch.

I looked at it too. "Yeah, so that happened," I muttered.

"It's huge," she said in a bland voice.

"Is it?" I didn't dare touch it. "Let's not talk about it, okay? I don't want it to, uh, get..." It twitched. I turned away from her, shifting uncomfortably on my feet.

"It looks like a human cock," she said. "Like a Toth one. Maybe you have a hairier foreskin, but—"

"I mean, we are all compatible with each other, so that would make sense."

"Except *huge*." This was an accusation. "Where is your pleasure cock?"

"It's, you know, tucked away."

"And you can't tuck that away?"

"It, like, the scrotum part just keeps knocking it—"

"Maybe put your pleasure cock in front of it."

"I don't think that makes any sense," I muttered. "I mean that's just going to stimulate my pleasure cock, and—"

"I don't want to *look* at it."

"Well, avert your fucking eyes!" I snapped.

She let out a trembling breath and then she was suddenly touching me, her hands were on me—

I snatched at her fingers, her wrists. I wasn't gentle. I forced her hands away. "*Stop.*"

She backed off, pulling her hands back. "No, you're right, that was fucked up. Just because your genitals are hanging out there like that doesn't mean I should feel as if I have the right to touch them." Her voice was shaking.

"Let's walk," I said in a measured, even voice.

"Yeah," she said. "Yeah, let's walk."

We walked.

I was hard. Just… it was happening. My cock was stiff and it was sticking out of me, and it felt… good.

But I breathed. I just breathed and breathed, and it… nothing happened. I didn't go insane. I didn't lose my head. I was simply turned on and thinking about all the blood that was rushing there and how it felt and I wasn't… I was fine.

I was in control.

Maybe this was going to be okay.

Maybe… maybe all the stuff about the crazed mating instinct had been exaggerated. Maybe I would not lose my head at all. Maybe I wouldn't force myself on her.

We walked and walked.

And then the ship came into view, and she saw it, and she clapped her hands and let out a whoop and she started running for it.

The sight of her like that, running through the woods, the shape of her hips and ass and legs, it—

My cock pulsed and I felt as if a spark of something traveled up my spine and burst right at the base of my skull.

I *had* to chase her.

TEN

cypra

I looked over my shoulder and he was coming for me, and he didn't look… sane.

There was some expression on his face, something that was single-minded and empty, *wild*. I should have called out his name or tried to communicate with him.

But somehow, I couldn't.

I could only do one thing.

Run faster.

I picked up my feet and careened through the trees, going around the ship now, out amongst the trunks of the trees which loomed up shadowy in the darkness. I ran as fast as I could, ran like my life depended on it.

And he caught me, because he was so much faster than me on those hooves of his. I'd thought before that he was like a blur.

He caught me and he pressed me face first into one of those tree trunks, and his very hard, very huge cock nudged itself between my legs, but I was wearing pants, and no matter what it was he was doing with that thing, it couldn't get *in* me.

I struggled.

"Stop," he managed in a garbled voice. "Still. Go still."

I obeyed him.

He panted into my neck. He rutted my crotch, poking into my pants-covered body at all sorts of points. And then he stopped and backed away. "Do not run," he ordered me in a gravelly voice.

I was still plastered against the tree. "Okay," I whispered.

"Okay," he said.

I looked over my shoulder.

He was backing up. His cock was jutting out from his body, and it was enormous and fully erect—thick and brown, the head of it a dark red color, almost crimson. It glistened. It was gorgeous.

I sagged against the tree.

He kept backing up.

I moved away from the tree.

He put his back to me.

Together, far apart, we made our way back to the ship.

But he didn't go in. He stood outside, shaking his head. "It'll be better if I stay out here, I think."

"Okay," I said in a breathy voice. "Okay."

The ship did not look wrecked. It was one of the rounded Thebe-K111s, which resembled nothing more than a flying disc—which is kind of funny, because I've been told humans used to call spaceships flying saucers, and it's possible that they were seeing these Thebe ships, but back then, when they weren't abducting women for breeding but just grabbing people for study and observation, they were probably the Thebe-K3s, which are older and you don't see as much of them anymore.

It was up on its landing wheels, which extended out of the disc, and it looked in pristine condition. I entered the query code I'd been given to open the hatch and it came down with a hiss.

I glanced back at Holston, who had his back to the ship now, staring out into the darkness.

Then I climbed aboard.

The hisec I got up inside the ship, I smelled something awful. It smelled like death. I grimaced, but I supposed I'd known that was likely what I was going to find here in the ship.

I began to walk up the corridor into the ship. As I walked, the motion-sensor lights came on, illuminating a small space in front of me a little bit at a time. As I walked, the stench grew stronger.

And then, a set of lights came on and illuminated a pool of blood. It wasn't large, maybe the size of my fist.

I got closer.

More blood. Drops of it.

It was a trail. Someone had been bleeding and had been going up this corridor.

I sucked in a breath. I thought about going back for Holston. He was the one with weapons. Even if he wouldn't come in with me, maybe he could loan me a knife.

But no.

This was my mission. I did not need him.

I sucked in another breath, this one determined, and I went faster, avoiding walking in the droplets of blood, but following the trail through the ship.

It took me to a closed door.

Someone's quarters.

I palmed the controls to open the door.

"Unknown occupant. Access denied," chirped the door.

"Override, code crimson," I said.

"Access code?"

"Five seven bravo eight echo," I said.

The door opened.

The stench hit me like a wave of awfulness.

There was a woman sprawled out on the bed. She was human. She was dead. She'd been shot with a blaster several times, and the trail of blood went to her bed. Her chest was a mass of pooling blood. She was curled up around her wound, cringing as if in pain. She must have bled out here.

I backed out of the room, shaking all over.

This… this wasn't what I'd expected.

I had thought that maybe the ship had crashed, and people had died when it went down or that maybe they'd left the ship and the vvoln had gotten them, but this?

Shot with a blaster?

This was murder.

And I was horrified, but I thought the signs pointed to it having been carried out by someone on the ship. Another member of the resistance.

What could have happened? I couldn't even imagine it.

I turned in a circle outside the door, struggling to think, to breathe. Well, I didn't know who'd done this, but there was a chance that the person who did was still alive on the ship, perhaps infected with some madness that made them murderous, and maybe I should get the weapon schematics and get the stars off the freaking ship before I got hurt too.

I stepped back into the quarters and approached the corpse.

She had a blaster in a holster strapped to her waist.

I eased it out and took out the power cartridge, checking to see if it was charged.

Mostly.

I slammed it back in.

When I left the room, I led with the blaster. It was a Falco-L10, the kind of hand blaster favored by law enforcement and security guards. It was lightweight but deadly, giving off a concentrated beam that could sizzle anything to death if it hit in the right place. I wondered why the woman in the room hadn't used it against her attacker.

On the other hand, maybe she had, I thought, because after I went a little further, I encountered another trail of blood, but this one was different. There was less of it, and some of it was smeared on the walls, as if someone had their hand in against a wound, trying to stanch the blood and had then used that hand to steady themselves.

I followed this trail all the way to the bridge of the ship, which was where I'd been headed anyway. I could access the stored schematics from here.

I found another corpse there.

This was a donen.

A donen? What was he doing on the ship? He was clothed. He had a shirt on and a pair of pants, but his clothing was full of blood, and he was sitting in one of the seats in the bridge clutching a blaster and gazing sightlessly out at the array of controls for the ship. His antlers weren't as tall or as numerous as Holston's. Did that mean he was younger?

His chin was resting against his chest.

I pushed past him and took off my bracelet. I tapped the side of it and a little nodule came out. I plugged my bracelet directly into the main control board of the ship and then I began tapping on the ship's control keyboard, looking around for the schematics I needed.

There.

Okay.

I moved the schematics over to the bracelet and then I snatched it back out and rushed back through the ship.

I climbed down and Holston was nowhere to be found.

But when I walked around the ship, I saw a fire.

I headed over and found it burning away merrily. He wasn't there either, but neither was his bolts and bow. He was hunting.

I gripped the blaster I had and sat near the fire and shook.

What was that donen doing there? Had he shot the woman in her quarters? How had he gotten on the ship?

Holston materialized out of the darkness, dragging a big bird. "I told you to stay on the ship."

"Do donen ever wear clothes?" I said.

"It's not safe out here." He gestured. "On the ship, you can keep both me and the vvoln out—"

"Like in the cities, maybe?"

"In the cities what?"

"Clothes," I said.

"No," he said, shaking his head. "I mean, okay, once in a long, long while, you'll see a donen on some vid or something, and they're always clothed. I figure it's like anything. You decide to leave your home planet, you got to assimilate."

I let out a breath. "Right. He must have been on the ship. He must have brought the ship down here. It makes sense. It's his planet. And I did think that it had to have been a member of the resistance who committed the murder—Can your mating madness affect a guy in space?"

"What are you talking about?"

"They're dead, on the ship," I said.

"I told you they would be."

"But dead because they were shot with blasters," I said.

He straightened up. "Seriously?"

"Come and look," I said, getting to my feet.

"Shei, I don't need to go on that ship—"

"You get really turned on by blood?"

"Uh, no?"

"Okay, then, I think it'll be fine. It smells horrible on that ship. Most unsexy thing ever."

He considered. He dropped the dead bird and the bolts and bow and he nodded at me. "Lead the way, shei."

I brought him onto the ship and he inspected both the bodies with me. He stood over the donen guy and looked him over. Then he reached down and tugged on the guy's pants.

"What are you doing?" I said.

"Looking to see if he..." He straightened. "It's not mating madness. His cock is not descended."

"Okay," I said. "I should have thought of that. Well, it's good to know you're not going to be murderous."

"Why would I kill you? How would that help me reproduce?"

"No, I..." I threw up my hands. "I'm just flustered." I backed out of the bridge. "Anyway, what are we going to do? It occurs to me that all we've done is plan to get to the ship, and we didn't make any plans for how to get back home."

"I guess I was figuring you could hole up here and I could fight my way back for help," he said.

"You can't leave me alone on a ship with corpses!"

"We'll get the corpses out and, uh, we'll clean, and it'll be fine."

"I wonder if the ship works," I said. "It doesn't look crashed. Can you fly a ship?"

"No," he said. "Can you?"

"No," I said.

"Well, then," he said.

I rubbed my forehead. "I don't want to be in here. Let me come and sleep by the fire with you. And I'm hungry. Can I have some of that bird?"

"You don't want to fire up the ship's replicator?" He grinned at me.

"Ugh, plastic-y flavored protein rations versus delicious food cooked over an open flame? No contest."

"So, you think I'm a good cook?" He was still grinning.

"You..." I threw up my hands again, and started for the exit of the ship.

"Shei, it's really dumb for you to be out in the open," he called after me.

"I don't care. I can't sleep on this ship. It's a coffin."

ELEVEN

cypra

I woke next to the fire to the thought that I had forgotten something very important. There had been three people on that ship, three members of the resistance, and I hadn't found the third member of the crew.

I sat up, and Holston was not sleeping on the other side of the fire.

Instead, a little ways off, I could see him crouched down, his head up, his antlers illuminated red-orange as they reflected in the flames. He turned to look at me, his head a jerking movement, animalistic.

I hunched up, fearful, instinctive.

"Don't run, shei," he said in a guttural voice.

I gulped.

A noise, off in the darkness, somewhere far away.

Holston's head jerked back in that direction.

Suddenly, I saw more antlers. Three pairs.

I sat up straight as three donen men materialized out of the darkness. They moved independently of each other, and they were all in a similar crouched position like Holston was.

Holston sniffed the air, and his eyes widened.

The men all started forward, galloping, fast, blurred movement. They were coming for *me*.

I stood up straight.

Holston shot out for them, another blur. "Cypra, run!" he cried.

I turned and took off, heading for the ship.

But I couldn't outrun a donen male. It was an impossibility.

One of them tackled me to the ground immediately.

I fought, struggling, bringing my elbows back into him.

He put a hand on my neck, holding me down. "Feisty thing," he said in a thick voice.

Oh, stars, he sounded like he was enjoying this.

Blaster!

I had a blaster, what was I thinking?

I fumbled for it. It was strapped to my waist, and I got it out.

He saw it. "Fuck!"

"Back off." I gestured wildly with the blaster.

He backed off.

I turned, still on the ground, holding the blaster, pointing it at him.

In the distance, I could see Holston's antlers locked in with another man's antlers, the two of them sparring with each other. Stars, I hoped he could take care of himself!

"Okay," I breathed. "I'm going into the ship, and you are going to—"

Movement.

The third donen man appeared, coming for me from my right side.

I jerked the blaster around and pulled the trigger.

Nothing happened.

The power cartridge! I hadn't charged it. I was such an idiot.

The third donen man tackled me, laughing.

I struggled against him.

He pressed his full weight onto me, and he seized my wrists and forced them up over my head. He pried the blaster out of my hands and tossed it off into the darkness.

I screamed.

The donen held onto both of my hands with one of his.

I tried to pull free, but he was too strong. I writhed, trying to buck him off with my body, trying to get a leg free, a foot, a knee, something.

His other hand went to the eazclasp of my pants. It parted. He tugged.

I screamed again. I was livid. I was nothing but anger. This was not *happening*.

I brought my head up into his face, driving my skull into his chin.

He shrieked.

Pain blossomed into my head. I cried out, tears streaming down my face.

And he was still holding *onto* me. That hadn't even made him loosen his grip.

He hit me.

An open handed slap across my face. It *hurt*.

I gasped up at him, quivering, terrified, despair blooming up from the depths of my body.

New plan, I was thinking frantically. *New plan, stay still, play dead. Maybe he'll just… just…*

What?

Oh, stars, how easily I was subdued. How easily the fight went out of me.

It's fine, I thought fiercely. *So, he fucks you, big fucking deal, you can deal with it. Look at the stars, just look up at the stars and think of something else.*

I let out a shaking breath and did exactly that.

But the second donen man yanked the third donen off of me.

I was too stunned to react.

The second donen man wrapped an arm around the third donen man's neck and twisted.

There was a crack.

I let out a gasp, and I sat up.

The second donen man tossed aside the corpse of the other man and came for me.

I…

I was frozen.

It was stupid. I knew it was stupid. I knew it, and yet I couldn't—

His hand tangled in my hair and he yanked my head back.

I tried to make noise, but nothing came out. I was shaking all over.

He ripped my pants.

I shut my eyes.

He turned me over, face into the ground.

I tensed, no thoughts, just waiting for it, waiting…

But there was nothing but air on my naked legs, between my legs.

And then there was another noise, a gurgling sort of noise, and I opened my eyes and turned around.

Holston had the second donen man. Holston's antlers were thrust into his neck.

I watched as Holston used his hooves to kick the man's lifeless body off, as he straightened up, towering over me, his antlers dripping blood. The other donen men were all dead. It was just him.

His cock was…

Oh, stars.

I bit down on my lip.

Should I run or would that mean he couldn't control himself? Could he control himself now?

He gazed down at me.

I was lying belly down on the ground with my pants ripped, my ass bare, twisting around to look at him looming over me. I let out a little noise, a kind of breathy noise of horror.

He went down on his knees.

"Holston?" I managed.

One of his big, warm hands landed on my ass cheek. His thumb delved into me, skimming the bud of my asshole, then down, sinking into me *there*.

And I was wet.

What the fuck was that?

I could *not* be wet. I was not excited by this, rape fantasies be damned—this was traumatic, and I didn't *want* this, not like this, not like—

He let out a rattling, noisy breath.

"Holston?" I whispered again, my voice pitiful. "Please."

"Mine," he rasped.

I shuddered.

Both of his hands on me now, pulling my body back against him. Somehow, he just... pulled my body directly onto his erection. It pierced me, huge and thick and overwhelming, filling up every inch of space inside my body, and I let out a little keening noise.

He moaned.

I shuddered again. It was too big. It was too much. I was split open and crammed full of him, and I was... I didn't...

He banded one arm around my waist and tugged me

up against his chest. He put his mouth on my spine, on my neck, on that spot where he'd bitten me before. But he didn't use his teeth, just his lips and tongue, and little of his nose, too. He panted against me.

"Holston." My voice was all stretched out and strained.

He grunted. He thrust into me. "I can't stop," he breathed. He spoke again, with effort, his voice garbled. "Touch yourself? Can you make it at least not… can you make yourself feel good?" His other hand went to one of my breasts and he gave it a gentle squeeze.

It was a dart of sweetness into my core.

He thrust again. His huge, thick cock dragged against something inside me, something good. It was intense, maybe it was too much—

I put my fingers on my clit.

He thrust again.

Now, it was like my clit was… was *trapped* between his driving cock and my finger. Oh, stars, I'd never felt *anything* like that in my life. I started to moan.

He grunted his approval at this, thrusting harder.

He fucked me desperately, a driving rhythm, slamming all the way into me, and I touched myself, and it *did* feel good.

He didn't last long, though.

I didn't come.

He finished, pumping me full of his sticky release and then he extricated himself from me, and he staggered away.

I wavered, left on my knees there. My whole body was shaking.

"Get up," he ordered from behind me, his voice like midnight. "Get onto the ship *now*."

I stumbled to my feet on trembling legs. I glanced at him over my shoulder.

He looked me up and down, the expression on his face hungry and possessive.

I took a shaky step toward the ship.

"Don't run," he warned me.

"No," I breathed. I walked, one careful step at a time, to the ship, while his semen slid slowly out of me.

TWELVE

holston

I brought Cypra food sometime later.

I wasn't sure what the agreed-upon apology for raping a woman was, but, well, this was what I had. I didn't want to make her look at me, so I just banged on the door of the ship, left it there, and pulled back out of sight.

But when she opened the door, she peered out. "Holston?" she called. "Is that you?"

I didn't say anything.

"Holston, did you bring this?" Real panic in her voice now.

"Yeah," I managed from my hiding place. "Yeah, I thought maybe… if you didn't want to use a replicator."

"Thank you," she said. "Where are you?"

"I'm sure you don't want to look at me," I muttered. I should have felt ashamed of myself for what happened. I probably would feel ashamed at some point, but the mating instinct was fucking up everything in my brain and body right now. So, it was more this feeling of knowing that shame was the appropriate reaction than it was that I felt anything at all.

"I need you to help me get the bodies out of the

ship," she said, voice breaking.

Shit.

"Can you be around me like that?"

Good question. I considered. "I don't know," I finally said.

She picked up the food and pulled it back inside the ship. "Um? There's someone else in here. She's alive but unconscious."

I came out from my hiding spot. "What?"

She flinched at the sight of me.

I pulled back, going back out of sight.

"No, wait," she said. "It's fine."

"It's obviously not fine." My voice was flat.

"Well..." She trailed off.

"Who else is on the ship?"

"She's Abbunian," she said.

"Okay," I said.

"From the planet of Abbunn," she said. "There's only one sentient species on that planet, and they're just called—well, anyway, she's in the sick bay and she's unconscious, so I don't know who she is or anything about her. But she's wounded. Looks like blaster shots. She was in the middle of trying to patch herself up when she passed out. Looks like she has a head injury. Maybe she fell or maybe someone hit her. I don't know. I finished tending the wounds she couldn't get to, but there's not much else I can do. The ship, though, it smells horrible on there, and I could really use the help getting the corpses off. Will you help?"

I hesitated, but then I looked up at her, gauging my body's reaction to looking at her. There was a surge of possessiveness and a feeling of protectiveness.

Mine.

But my cock didn't so much as twitch, which was a

relief. That thing was…

It didn't even feel like part of me. It was some strange appendage that was now attached to me with a mind of its own. I didn't like it.

"I can help," I said, sucking in a breath through my nose. "What I'll do is just… do it. I'll get them off the ship. You… go elsewhere."

She bit down on her lip. "Is it… you can't… you're out of control still?"

"I'm not myself," I said.

She blinked at me. "What's that mean?"

"It started when I scented you," I said. "I've been making decisions that I'd never make, behaving in ways I never would. I know what I should do, but it's like… I don't do it."

"Well, that's the whole time we've been together," she said. "It's worse now?"

"Yeah."

"But you're not… you're talking to me. You're not out of your head. You seem—"

"Well, I'm not." My voice came out sharper than I meant it to.

She flinched again.

"Just… go hide somewhere," I muttered. "I'll take care of the corpses."

"I can help," she said.

"I owe you, right?" I said. "Besides, probably safer if we're not near each other."

She shifted on her feet, looking down at the roasted meat I'd brought her. She didn't go anywhere.

This annoyed me, but maybe just because I was easily frustrated right now. "Cypra, *go*."

"Now you're mad at me?" She looked up at me, reproachful.

"No," I said, too much protest in it. "What do you care? I'm sure you hate me."

It was quiet again.

She took a step backwards. Stopped. Looked up at me again. "Did you like it?"

I knew what she meant. She meant, did I like fucking her? "Of course not."

She drew back at this, as if this had hurt her feelings or something.

Lose me in deep space, what was *that?* "I mean, it felt good or whatever, but it was horrible, all of it. I just don't like being that guy, being selfish, *using* you. I wanted to want to stop. Like really wished I cared, but I... I fucking hate myself. Go *away.*"

She twisted her hands together. "I, um, I kind of liked it?"

I drew back, horrified.

"I mean, not really." She glanced up at me, saw the look on my face, and looked away with a shudder. "Never mind," she whispered, and then she scurried off into the ship.

"Don't run!" I yelled after her, my voice thick.

"Sorry." She glanced at me over her shoulder, wincing again. She slowed. She disappeared into the ship.

I stood there, breathing too hard. I had another thought about shame. If I were myself, I'd feel ashamed of making her feel bad about running, because that was fucked up. It was on me, not her. I shouldn't blame *her* for what *I* did.

I scratched one of my antlers, trying to summon a feeling of actual shame or actual regret. It was gone. I didn't apparently have the capacity for such things right now. My cock descended and I became, like, a sociopath? A sociopath rapist.

This was *perfect*.

I put my head down and stalked onto the ship.

I was glad of the distraction of hard, heavy, disgusting work. Pulling the bodies off the ship gave me something to do, and it was all-consuming. I didn't have to concentrate on anything else other than wrapping them up in sheets I found in storage compartments, dragging them out, and burying them.

If I'd cared about anything at all, I would have asked Cypra if she wanted to say anything over their bodies.

But, all things considered, I didn't.

Once it was done, I knew I should just disappear, leave her be, but perversely, I sought her out.

She was in the sick bay sitting opposite the bed where the unconscious alien was sprawled out. The alien had horns that curled around her face. The rest of her body was covered in a sheet. She looked peaceful at least.

"Bodies are buried," I said to Cypra, looking her over where she was sitting.

Mine, I thought again, and I wanted to touch her.

I tried to tell myself not to.

But I didn't listen, because I was a sociopath now, so I went over and traced a finger down the line of her jaw.

She sucked in a breath and looked up at me with wide eyes.

"I'm not myself," I said in a gravelly voice. "I'm sorry about this." I didn't stop touching her. "You just… you feel like you belong to me."

She sucked in another sharp breath and gazed up at me with half-lidded eyes. "Do I?" she whispered.

I nodded.

"Not in here," she said, standing up, colliding with me, pressing her chest into mine.

I slid my hand into her hair. "I can't... I can't stop." This was a lie. I could totally stop. I just didn't *want* to stop, and I didn't seem to have any of the requisite emotions that would *make* me stop.

"Not *here.*" She shoved my chest.

I stumbled backwards.

She looked me over and then her eyes lit up and her lips curved into a mischievous smile. She darted away from me.

She *ran.*

Fuck.

I went after her.

I caught her in the hallway. I grabbed her and pulled her body back against mine and burrowed my nose against her neck, breathing in the scent of her. "That wasn't very smart, shei."

She wriggled into me, sighing. Then she batted at my hands on her hips. "Let go."

I didn't want to. But I tried hard, even if I couldn't feel shame, to remember that I knew shame was bad. *I'm going to really, really regret this if I don't stop,* I said to myself. And I let go of her, noisy air whooshing out of my nose as I did.

She turned, backing away from me. But she didn't move down the corridor. Instead, she backed into the wall.

"Shei..." I took a step toward her. "Don't trap yourself. What are you doing?"

"Get your pleasure cock out," she said, shimmying out of her pants. Her face was flushed, and when she removed her clothes, I got a scent of her there, and she smelled of arousal and want and of *me,* because I'd come in her before. My eyes rolled back in my head.

I didn't get anything out. My mating cock got hard as anything in the whole of the galaxy, and I went for her.

She put her hands on my crotch, squeezing my mating cock, stroking it, and her little fingers were…

"Fuck," I moaned, halting, transfixed by the sensation.

Then I felt her freeing my pleasure cock, stroking it, too, and I let out a low, affected groan.

She pulled me closer. She offered me her mouth.

I kissed her.

She hitched up a leg, wrapping her thigh around my hip.

I braced her up against the wall.

She reached between us, arranging my pleasure cock where she wanted it.

Fuck, she was wet, and that felt phenomenal.

Then she tucked my mating cock inside her body, and she was soft and slippery and snug and wondrous. I broke the kiss to make a noise—an indescribable, embarrassing noise. Except embarrassment was one of those emotions I didn't feel anymore, so I didn't *care*.

But she made one too, as I breached her, invaded her, filled her, and she threw back her head, rubbing her skull against the wall, her eyes shut.

I put my mouth on her jaw. On her cheekbone. On her temple. I thrust into her.

She kept making noise. Lose me, those noises turned me *on*. My hips worked into her, my body slamming against her, as if moving of its own volition. It knew how to do this, but I didn't seem to be making real conscious decisions about my movement.

She reached between us, finding my pleasure cock.

I cried out.

"Here," she gasped. "Right here." She moved it, putting it where she wanted it. "There. That's good."

"Is it?" I panted.

"Mmm," she said. "Make me come, Holston. Don't you *dare* come before me."

My eyes snapped open and I pulled back to meet her gaze. Oh, fuck, that turned me on.

She gave me a fierce smile.

"Cypra," I breathed. This woman, she… it was different than her being mine, suddenly, it was reciprocal. I was hers. I wanted to be hers anyway. I cared about her pleasure—and that didn't seem entirely sociopathic to me, after all. Huh.

"Don't you dare," she repeated.

"Whatever you say," I said, but I didn't even know how to fulfill that. This was precisely the second time my mating cock had ever ejaculated—okay, well, I hadn't come yet, but I was going to—and to think I had any kind of control over it, finesse with it, it was ludicrous.

But displeasing her was also not an option.

So, she just needed to come quickly, really quickly, because I could not hold this back, no way. I put my hands on her breasts, finding her nipples, remembering the way I'd teased them before, how they'd responded to me, hoping I could do that again, and they rewarded me by stiffening right away when my fingers found them.

She sighed at my touch.

I could feel the rhythm of my pleasure cock against her clit, and I tried to time the strokes of my fingers on her nipples with it, tried to make it all move with my thrusts, somehow, as if I was tapping into something ancient and powerful, some force that moved in and through us both, something as old as the stars themselves.

I was concentrating so hard on her, I realized I'd stopped focusing on my own pleasure, and I might have actually stalled off my orgasm.

Oh, shit.

No. I hadn't, I hadn't at all, and—

It was an explosion, a tightness that started in my balls and shot through me, shot out of me. There were tight little jerks as I expelled it all.

"Lose me in deep space, I'm sorry," I muttered. Fuck, fuck, fuck.

"Did you just come?" She was not pleased.

"I..."

"What's happening to your pleasure cock? Does it get soft with your mating cock?"

"I don't *know,*" I said. "I guess?"

She narrowed her eyes at me.

"Look, I'll..." I slid my soft member out of her and dropped to my knees. "I'll make it up to you."

Her eyes widened.

I put my mouth on her clit. I licked, trying to make my tongue do what my pleasure cock did, trying to find that rippling movement that she liked.

She grabbed onto my antlers and moaned.

I licked like a wild man. I loved the way she tasted. I knew I was tasting myself on her, seeping out of her, and that... maybe that was kind of dirty or gross or something, but I didn't care. To me, it just seemed hotter, because it was more of the way I'd claimed her, more indication that she was mine, and obviously I should taste myself there.

What I wanted, basically, was to have her filled full

of my seed all the time, so that it was dripping out of her pretty little pussy constantly, because she was mine, mine, mine.

Her pussy was mine, and I was going to lick it until she screamed.

Which she did.

For a long time.

She screamed and sighed and cursed, and jerked my head around by tugging on my antlers, and I licked her and licked her and licked her.

And finally, finally, she convulsed against me, sobbing and sagging into the wall.

I kept licking until she shoved me away, using my antlers to do that, too, and then I collapsed in a heap and gazed up at her, at her bare, dripping pussy and her heaving breasts and her closed eyes and she was the most beautiful woman in the *universe*. "I'm yours," I said hoarsely. "Do whatever you want with me."

She opened her eyes in slits and giggled. "Holston…"

I shook my head. I groaned. "What am I saying?"

"You're taking it back?" She was disappointed.

"I'm just… that was… did you consent to that?"

"*Yes.*"

"But I mean, really? Because, I think you just accepted it as an inevitability and decided to make the best of it."

She giggled again. She came over and offered me her hand.

I took it. I let her help me to my feet.

She wound my arm around her shoulders.

We walked down the corridor like that.

She guided us into a room where there was a narrow bed, and she lay down on it and tugged me down with her.

I wrapped my body around hers.

She took off her shirt, muttering something about comfort. She yawned. "Nap?"

"Nap," I breathed. I was tired too. I burrowed down into her. I usually found sleeping in the same bed with another person uncomfortable, and I would pull away and roll over to sleep unencumbered, but she felt like the lost part of me I hadn't known that I was missing, and I fell asleep against the soft wonder of her breasts, and it was perfection.

* * *

cypra

I woke up with Holston's antlers in my face, and I grabbed them and pushed his head away.

He sighed, rolling over onto his back, and stayed asleep.

Of course he did. The man could sleep through *anything*.

I peered down at his sleeping face.

Well, this is all fucked up, Cypra, I said to myself. What were all these weird tender feelings I was developing for him? Should I be doing that?

You should not, I answered myself.

I traced a finger over one of his antlers.

He shivered and jerked away, eyes fluttering.

This made me giggle.

He opened his eyes again, taking me in. "You're still naked," he said.

I snorted.

He shut his eyes, snuggling back into the pillow, a satisfied smile stealing over his features. "Best way to wake up ever."

Oh. That was… that made my stomach do a little

flip. I liked him. I liked him liking me. I liked him not being able to resist me and having to have me so badly that he couldn't hold back from doing it. I liked him with his face between my thighs, tongue going at me like I was something delicious. I liked him being mine, like he said he was.

Obviously, it was bullshit.

He couldn't help it. He was riding some mating instinct thing and he wanted me because I was there, and it didn't mean anything.

It had been this way all along.

Hadn't I said it to him, that my attraction was genuine and his was forced?

So, in the end, which of us was being raped, him or me?

He seemed pretty concerned about forcing himself on me, but I... he was being forced by his biology. At least I wasn't forcing him. I mean, I wasn't necessarily trying to stop it, but I *couldn't*. He was stronger than me and I *had* to let him.

I mean... didn't I?

Was I trying very hard to stop him?

He cupped one of my breasts, possessive, gentle. He opened his eyes, still smiling that shit-eating grin, like he'd won a prize or something.

I felt melty.

"You're beautiful," he whispered, his voice deep and sleep-ravaged.

I kissed him.

He rolled on top of me to deepen the kiss.

We kissed and kissed and his cock got hard.

He winced. "Sorry about that?"

"No, it's okay," I said. "Maybe if we just, um, tend to you there it'll help you stay in control?"

"Uh..." He ran his nose down my neck, down, down, down, down, between the cleft of my breasts.

I writhed, basking, throwing my arms over my head. "Do you want me?"

"You know I do," he rasped.

"I'm yours," I murmured.

He groaned. He took one of my nipples between his lips. He teased it there, making it hard, making little shocks of pleasure shoot through my body, and then he licked the tip of it. He pulled back to survey his handiwork.

I sighed, pressing my pelvis up into his, rolling my hips into his hardness.

He kissed my very stiff nipple. "Let's just go on the record here that you're, uh, you're not mine. You don't belong to anyone except yourself—"

"Stop," I grunted.

"Let's just go on the record that I know this is wrong." He sucked my sensitive flesh into his mouth.

I writhed, sighing at the sensation that flooded me. It felt so good. "Maybe so," I managed. "Maybe it's wrong."

He lifted his face and looked at me.

"Can we pretend it's not?" I said. "We can't stop, so, let's just... pretend."

He lowered his face to my other nipple and licked it too.

It went immediately stiff and thrills went through me. I gasped. "Pretend I'm yours. Pretend you're mine."

"You're sure you're all right with that, shei?"

"It's wrong, but it feels good." I arched my back, pushing my breast against him, offering it to him.

He claimed it, suckling it roughly.

I cried out. "Yours," I said. "Make me yours with your *cocks*."

He grunted. "I want to come in you, shei. I want you overflowing with me. I want to be dripping out of you constantly. Keep your pussy filled up."

"Please," I said, my whole body tightening at the thought of it. "Please, Holston, fuck me. Just keep fucking me again and *again*."

His mouth found mine.

We kissed frantically, mouths wet and eager against each other, until he pulled away and ordered me in a raw voice to put his pleasure cock on my clit just how I liked it, and I did, and then he ordered me to put his mating cock inside me, his voice breaking when he said it felt good when I touched him and tucked him inside, and I was so turned on that I came two minutes into his pleasure cock rubbing my clit, and then he erupted inside me while I was coming.

Afterwards, he lay on top of me, the heaviness of his body pressing me into the bed, his cock softening but still inside me, and I thought he was going to fall asleep like that, and I kind of wanted him to, even though he was maybe too heavy.

But he suddenly pushed up on his arms over me, and this tugged his penis out of my body, and I made a little disappointed noise, and he rocked backwards, on his knees at the foot of the bed and gazed at me with greedy eyes. "This is fucked up," he said.

"I thought we were going to pretend—"

"Shei, we can't just ignore all of the problems we have right now and, uh, have some kind of orgy."

"I think orgies need more than two people." I propped myself up on my elbows.

"You know what I mean."

I sighed. "By problems, you mean, where the stars did those other three donen men come from? What if someone realizes you killed them? Are they going to be mad? Who killed the two dead people on this ship and wounded the Abbunian? That kind of stuff?"

He nodded, reaching up to worry at the tip of one of his antlers. "Not to mention the big one. How do we get out of here?" He looked at me again. "Can you, uh, would you mind getting dressed?"

"*You* never get dressed," I said.

He looked down at his mating cock. "Well, I mean, this is sort of ugly and I'm sure it doesn't arouse you—"

"*Yes,* it does."

He fixed me with a look.

Then we were suddenly kissing again.

In between, he gasped into my mouth, "You like looking at my mating cock, shei?"

"I do, I do. It's a very pretty cock, and every time I see it, I want to touch it."

He groaned, pressing me back into the bed, driving his pelvis into me again.

I felt him harden again and I writhed into his erection.

He peeled himself off me and went to the other side of the room. "I don't think tending to this is making it any less, uh, responsive."

I beckoned him. "Well, maybe we should thoroughly test that theory," I said.

He leaned against the far wall, head down, antlers sticking out, and he gazed darkly at me from beneath them. "Don't."

I eyed his very hard cock and thought about going over there and getting on my knees and returning the favor from when he'd licked me so very thoroughly.

"Okay, look, I'll put on pants," he said, pushing off from the wall. He left the room.

I sat up on the bed and sighed. Where were my clothes?

His voice came from the hallway. "You think you could help me find something on this ship? Where did the dead guy keep his clothes?"

"I don't know!" I called back. I got out of the bed, rolling my eyes. "Just because I'm a woman, I'm supposed to be better at finding things?"

"Well, you've been on this ship for longer, and it's a resistance ship, so you're probably more familiar with the layout, and—"

"Okay, fine, I'll help you." I shrugged into my clothes and came out into the corridor.

He turned to me, and his cock was still sticking straight out.

I swallowed visibly.

He let out a soft laugh. "Uh, so… you really do find me arousing?"

"Obviously." I walked past him, annoyed.

He fell into step with me. "*Am* I forcing you, shei?"

"No," I said.

"But you agreed with me that it was wrong."

"*You're* being forced," I said.

"No, I'm not," he said.

"You are," I said. "You told me that you're not yourself, and that you haven't been since you scented me. And before I forced you to come to this stupid ship, you told me you only wanted to go home, and I didn't let you—"

"Hey," he said, putting a hand on my shoulder. "I'm *fine*."

I stopped walking and looked up at him.

He looked down at me.

"Wait until this passes, and then you decide if you're fine," I said.

His fingers traveled up my neck to brush over my cheek. "This can't hurt me. I'll be fine. But, uh, we've never figured out... if there is something wrong with your implant—"

"There's not."

"But then why did your scent—"

"Just... that's ridiculous," I said. "We're both on suppressants to keep our biology in check so that we can't reproduce and both of them are failing at the same time? That doesn't happen. It's contrived, like a horrible plot device on some awful holovid. I mean, what are the odds?"

"If I get you pregnant—"

"No," I said.

"Well, you should terminate," he said, letting his hand drop. "And I'm really sorry that I seem to have some weird fetish with coming inside you." He started walking again.

"I'm not going to get pregnant," I called after him. "Let's not talk about that."

He kept walking.

"Obviously, I would terminate," I said. "But that wouldn't even be your decision."

"No," he said, still walking. "It would not. But it's why you should worry about yourself and not me. There are no consequences for me."

My shoulders slumped. I looked down at my flat stomach and I felt a hot ball of anxiety tighten around my spine.

I was *not* going to get pregnant.

THIRTEEN

holston

I did not like wearing pants.

They felt strange, and they made the fur on my legs itch, and they seemed more stimulating on my mating cock, which meant that I was straining against them most of the time.

But I forced myself not to think about that, and to focus on the most pressing problems we had instead.

"It's impossible to repair that tire," I said. "We can't get the speeder out of here, so that's out. I still think our best bet is for me to leave and go for help."

"What if there are more donen men out there?" she said. "What if they scent me out and find some way to break onto the ship? It's not impenetrable, you know."

"Yeah, I guess when I made that plan, I was thinking that you needed protection against the vvoln," I said. "They wouldn't be smart enough to know where to find the weak parts."

"Or to download unlock codes to their bracelets," she said.

"That's a thing?" I had never heard of such a thing.

"If you know where to look, absolutely."

I made a face. "Well, that doesn't make me feel very secure." I shrugged. "Of course, I usually don't lock my doors anyway." A pause. "I could bring you with me?"

"We'll fuck," she said. "And that scent will bring vvoln and maybe more donen men who are trying to take me from you. If they're out there, they'll come for me?"

I nodded. "But there can't be that many more of them. There's no way that many people are so stupid to come up here in Star Season."

"Well, I've been thinking about it," she said, "and the fact that those three came after me makes me think it's not like we thought. It's not like couples with a kink. Because if they had women they were going after, those women would have let their men catch them. They wouldn't have let them come after me like they did."

"What motivates people to risk their lives for sex?" I said. "Who does that?"

"Maybe it's not about sex," she said. "Maybe it's about something else. Something they believe in."

I thought about how I had thought that both of us were willing make sacrifices for things we found important. That I was willing to do a dangerous, difficult, uncomfortable activity just for the gratification of having conquered it. That she was willing to put everything on the line for the resistance.

But this was *really* dangerous. Our risks didn't compare to coming up here in Star Season.

"Maybe it's, like, almost a religion or something," she said. "Do you have any fanatical religions on Ohkk?"

I considered.

"Something obsessed with restoring the old ways or something," she said. "Coming up here was a fertility *rite*, wasn't it? It was a ceremonial, spiritual ritual."

"I guess." I nodded. "Yeah, I guess it was. And there

was this nonsense about various entities in the stars and stuff like that? The stars made us horny for each other, essentially. Our ancestors didn't know it was pollen in plants."

"So? Are there any groups like that?"

I shrugged. "There could be. I don't pay attention to that kind of thing." I furrowed my brow. "Some people can get really intense about religious stuff, like to the point where they're willing to die for it."

"They did die for it," she said. "They tried to take your mate, and you killed them for it."

I shifted on my feet. "That's, uh, you know... I don't just go around killing people every day."

"You okay?"

"Yeah, totally okay." I nodded. "Yeah, I don't feel *anything* about that. But my ability to feel shame or regret, it's kind of *off*."

She nodded slowly. "That's probably normal."

"Normal?"

"Well, when *any* species is turned on, we have a lesser capacity for those sorts of emotions. I think it's necessary, because otherwise, we'd probably not mate at all. It's a sort of gross and humiliating kind of activity, what with all the fluids and nudity? Arousal has to override those sorts of emotions or a species will die out. It's probably just more pronounced with you?"

That actually made sense. I was driven to pass on my genetic material, and anything that would get in the way of that—like feeling ashamed over killing competitors—needed to go if I was to be successful. Natural selection would ensure that those of us who did lose our shame were the most likely to breed and so the trait would be passed on.

"Did you really like it the first time?" I couldn't

believe she did. She'd been terrified. I'd smelled her fear. Admittedly, her fear scent had made me even more aroused, which was very, very fucked up, but I guessed that must also be part of it, of the thing we were talking about.

"It was intense," she said.

"Good intense? Really?"

"No." She furrowed her brow. "Not exactly good. Kind of traumatizing, actually, but, um, not as bad as it should have been either. Just... intense. And I don't feel anything toward you like I'd feel if you'd assaulted me, so I don't think you did."

"But... would you? Like, maybe it's some weird psychological survival thing. If you're traumatized, maybe it's a coping mechanism."

She considered. "It's possible."

"I need to keep my hands off of you and my cock out of you," I said.

"Well... maybe, but..."

"I really don't think I will, though," I muttered.

"Good," she said, squaring her shoulders. "Let's stop talking about it and just accept the fact we're fucking for the duration?"

"Yeah," I said. "Okay."

We were quiet.

"There seems to be an exception," she said.

"What are you talking about?"

"Your shame and regret?" she said. "It's still on when it comes to me."

"No, it's not or I'd stop fucking you," I said.

"But you care," she said. "Maybe just because I'm your, um, your mate, and you need to protect me in case of, uh, of offspring."

"Yeah, right," I said. "I guess that makes sense."

"Didn't you say that when your ancestors would come up here, they'd protect their women from competitive males? They'd probably also, uh, you know, try to keep the women with them by making them comfortable however they could," she said.

"I'm *not* making you comfortable."

"Well, you..." She sighed at me. "You do *care* about my comfort." A pause. "Don't you?"

I sighed again, looking at her. "Shei, I do... I feel..."

She nodded. "Me too."

It got quiet again.

She cleared her throat. "You, uh, think there are any tutorials in the ship's downloaded files on emergency takeoff or landing? Maybe flying this ship out of here is going to be our best bet."

"We can look," I said.

"Yeah, we should," she said.

But we didn't.

We went back to the bedroom and took off my pants and took off her pants and her shirt and spent a long time touching the sensitive parts of each other's bodies before I spread her thighs and held them open and told her that she was going to have to show off her pussy to me like this whenever I wanted her to.

And she said she thought that it was too empty and that she was due for me to fill her back up with my come.

Which made me kind of lose it, and I slammed into her and fucked her hard and fast, making her pretty breasts jiggle like crazy as I jerked in and out of her and as she moaned and begged.

I came before she did again and went down on her afterward, loving the salty mingling of our tastes. I growled into her pussy, demanding she tell me that she belonged to me, and she said it again and again in a high-pitched voice that broke.

I'm yours, I'm yours. Holston, I'm yours.

* * *

cypra

I was tucked in against his body, laying my cheek against his shoulder while his arm curved possessively around me, his hand resting on my hip. I had my thighs wrapped around his furry thigh, and I felt like we were all tangled up.

I kept having these odd sensations while we were touching each other, like I couldn't figure out where the boundaries were between us, like we had accidentally started spilling into each other, like we were part of each other now.

It was heady and good.

I was frightened of it.

I knew it wasn't real.

Chemicals, I told myself. *There are chemicals released in the brain during sex, during orgasms.*

I knew it didn't mean anything.

But I wasn't sure if that was going to make it hurt any less when this was all over.

He kissed my forehead. "Why did you sigh like that?"

Because I seem to be falling in love with you – chemically – and it's inconvenient. "No reason."

"You'd tell me if I was hurting you."

"I would." But sometimes it did sort of hurt, because his cock was very big, but it was a good hurt, the *best* kind of hurt, and I was sore, too, but the soreness was its own kind of deliciousness. I'd tell him if the hurt became so much that it drowned out my pleasure, that was what I meant.

"So, what's wrong?"

"Absolutely nothing. It was a good sigh." I sighed again, to punctuate my point.

He chuckled, sounding happy. "It's like that for me, too. Everything's kind of perfect right now."

I snuggled into him.

"You're… I've never been this attracted to a woman in my life."

I sighed again. It was chemicals making him feel that, too, but I didn't care. It was nice to hear. "I think you're great also, you know. And very attractive."

"Especially, you're attracted to my cock," he said, sounding pretty pleased by that.

"Yes," I agreed in a throaty voice. "Your cock is very, very nice. To look at, and to touch, and to feel inside me. But I'm partial to your pleasure cock, too."

"Because it makes you come," he said, tightening his grip on me.

"Well, *sometimes* it does," I said pointedly. "When someone can keep from being *premature*."

He chuckled again, nuzzling the top of my head. "I'm not worthy of you, shei."

"I don't know. You do redeem yourself admirably."

"I want to make you happy," he said. "I wish I could make you half as happy as you make me."

Don't say things like that. "You don't think I'm as happy as you are?"

"I don't think you could be. I'm delirious."

You're just going to make this harder, Holston. I burrowed my face into his skin. "That's only because you're hopped up on whatever chemical cocktail your brain is making to make you mate me," I muttered. "None of this is real."

He sighed. "Shit."

I moaned into his skin.

He stroked the back of my hair. "No, you're right, shei. This will all wear off. And we'll get out of this somehow, even if we're stuck here for the entire Star Season. And then you'll go back to your life with the resistance, and I'll go back to my life here, and…"

"Let's not talk about this either," I groaned.

"There's a lot of things you don't want to talk about."

"A lot of things are very fucked up!"

"It's only, it feels—"

"I *know* that."

He sighed. He let go of me.

I rolled away from him.

It was quiet.

"Sorry," he said finally.

I sat up. "No, don't be sorry. I'm the one who said we should pretend. I should have gone with it." I rubbed my forehead. "Give me a second, and I'll figure out a way to do exactly that. Pretend."

"Maybe we shouldn't," he sighed. He sat up too and he kissed the top of my shoulder. "All of this is bad enough without lying to ourselves about it all."

This hit me hard for some reason. My throat went tight and painful, and I had to fight the tears that stung my eyes.

"Shei, I'm so sorry about this," he murmured. "I'm so—"

"Don't," I said in a very strained voice. I got up from the bed and yanked on my clothes. "I'm going to check on the Abbunian woman."

He nodded slowly. "Yeah, I guess that's a good thing to do."

I palmed the controls and the door slid open with a

whoosh, but I hesitated before going out into the corridor. I turned to look at him. "If we go back now, get away from the pollen influence, will you…?" I nodded at his now-soft penis, which was lying against his leg.

"Uh, you mean, will the rut end?"

I nodded.

He shrugged. "I have no idea about that."

I looked down at my bracelet ruefully. "You don't realize how much you miss the networks until you can't reach them."

He chuckled. "I'm used to it, I guess." He was always up here, hunting things, living in the woods.

It was true that there wasn't any kind of future for us, even if I did… even if I was… well, it *was* chemicals, but even if it wasn't, there was no way we could make a life together. We were independent sorts of people. He had his hunting thing. I had the resistance. He'd even tried to equate them that one time around the fire. I didn't think hunting was anything remotely like what I did, but it was important to him.

I went into the corridor and headed for the sick bay.

I couldn't help but indulge in a stupid fantasy of us meeting up now and again. Maybe once every few gemoons, we could figure out a way to see each other, to be together…

But that was dumb.

He wouldn't even want me. He only wanted me because of his biological mating needs, and if we did hook up, he'd be on suppressants, and he wouldn't even have a cock—

Well, that pleasure cock of his…

No.

Stop thinking about this, Cypra, I urged myself.

When I got to the sick bay, the Abbunian woman was gone.

FOURTEEN

holston

I scrambled back on the bed, holding up both hands. "Don't shoot!"

The Abbunian woman from the sick bay lowered her blaster. "You're not Grilin."

"No," I said. "My name's Holston, and—"

"You're a donen, though."

"You're on a planet of donens," I said.

She narrowed her eyes at me, lifting the blaster again.

I stiffened. "Please, I'm not trying to hurt you. I swear, I have no intention of that."

"What are you doing on this ship?"

"I'm the guide," I said.

"The guide?"

"You're with the resistance, right? They sent someone after you, but she couldn't get up here on her own, and she hired me to get her up here."

The Abbunian regarded me.

"Uh, what's your name?" I said.

She gestured with the blaster. "So, where is this other person, then?"

"She went to check on you in the sick bay," I said. "Her name is Cypra. She's human."

The Abbunian looked me over, gaze settling on my

genitals. She raised her eyebrows.

I scrambled to cover myself. "Uh, sorry, I'm not used to having to worry about that."

"I'm Jini," she said. "I didn't think donen had external, um, I thought you were one of the cock pocket species." She winced. "Sorry. I guess that's not really an appropriate thing to..."

"Can you take that blaster off me?"

She holstered it. "I guess if I've seen your penis that breaks the ice, right? Let's be friends." She snickered, looking out into the corridor. "Is Grilin alive? I thought I got him pretty good, but I couldn't say."

"He was the other donen?" I said. "No. He's gone. Why'd, uh, why'd you shoot him?" *Are you going to shoot me, too?*

"He shot me first," she said. "And he killed Panna."

"So, it *was* him," I said softly.

"He went crazy," she said.

"Huh," I said. It couldn't have been mating madness. What set that guy off? "Well, you've been unconscious for a long time."

"Yeah." She rolled her shoulders. "I was in and out, actually. I wondered how I ended up hooked up in the sick bay. But if you did that, I should thank you, I guess. Saved my life."

"Cypra did that," I said.

Jini leaned out of the doorway. "You must be Cypra."

Cypra's voice carried down the corridor. "You're awake."

Jini backed out into the corridor too. "We can go to the lounge to talk." She glanced in at me. "You can come too. After you put some pants on."

Right. Pants. Great.

By the time I got down there, the two women were sitting opposite each other in chairs, each with steaming cups of replicator coffee.

"So, you can fly the ship?" Cypra was saying. "We're saved."

Jini looked up as I approached. "How'd you two get up here?"

"Speeder," I said. "But we had a tire blowout and it's useless. Can you fly the ship?"

"I'm not the admii," said Jini. "Grilin was. I have no idea why he took us down here. But if this is his home planet, like you said, maybe that's why."

"So, you can't fly the ship?" I said.

At the same time, Cypra said, "It was the donen guy after all? But he wasn't in a rut, so why?"

Jini looked back and forth between us. "I'm not an admii, but I can probably get the ship off the ground, and if I could fly it somewhere, like to a commercial spaceport, where they take over the controls and do the landing remotely for you, then... I mean, yeah, I can get us out of here. But is it an emergency or something? Why didn't the resistance send a ship?"

"Magnetic interference from the pole," said Cypra. "This Grilin guy started opening fire on you guys?"

"Well, at first he stunned us," said Jini. "He locked me and Panna up in a closet and we woke up and got out of there and started shooting at him, and that's when he started shooting back."

"Why?" said Cypra.

"He didn't really sit down and talk to us about it," said Jini.

"Look, it kind of doesn't matter," I said. "I'm as curious about it as anyone, but we can ponder it from elsewhere."

"Which brings us back to the question of whether it's an emergency," said Jini. "Because I can probably get around that magnetic interference and get our coordinates to the resistance. They'll come and get us."

"Oh," said Cypra. She looked up at me. "Well, I mean, if the resistance comes for you and me, that's fine, but Holston needs—"

"I'm fine up here," I said.

Cypra stood up, coffee sloshing out of her cup. "You're not. You're in a rut. And there are possibly more donen men out there. What do we think about them, that they're in a weird fertility cult or something? Is that what we said? And if that one woman we saw who got killed by that vvoln is any indication, then there could be other women. You go out there, you'll scent one, and you'll have to fight off whatever other man who's already claimed her, and he might kill you, or a vvoln might get you, or—"

"I'm fine," I said. "I can take care of myself. That's why you hired me."

"But it's my fault you're in the rut," she said. "I can't let you—"

"It's my fault for forgetting my suppressant," I countered.

"What's a rut?" said Jini.

Cypra and I both turned to look at her.

"I mean, no, it's okay," said Jini, glancing at my crotch. "I think I can mostly put that together for myself. What are vvoln?"

"Nasty tusked predators that like to play with their food," said Cypra, sitting back down in her chair.

"Okay, but we're safe from mindless predators in the ship," said Jini. "What's this fertility cult thing?"

"They're in the rut too," said Cypra. "Some of them

came for me. They tried to…" She looked away. "Anyway, they're dead now, but there might be more of them."

"They tried to, like, mate you?" said Jini. "Because that's what a rut is?" She looked at my crotch again.

I was starting to feel uncomfortable. And I was getting hard, which didn't make any sense, at least I didn't think it did. Discomfort and arousal should not happen at the same time. It was confusing.

Cypra nodded, gulping some of her coffee. Her voice was low. "But they didn't. They didn't do anything at all to me."

"Uh huh," said Jini. "Why is it your fault that Holston is, um, in a rut?"

"It's not," I said.

"We're not leaving him," said Cypra.

"We can get him on a transport back home," said Jini. "The resistance will arrange that for him. I'm sure that can be dealt with."

"Look," I said, "I'm not going into space on this ship just because—"

"You *are,*" said Cypra sharply. "I can't stand it if something happens to you."

Not entirely pretend, then. Maybe not for either of us. I hung my head and worried at one of the tips of my antlers. "All right. Whatever." I turned and walked out of the room.

* * *

cypra

I was on the bridge, chewing on my bottom lip as Jini sat at one of the consoles, furiously typing on one of the keyboards and staring up at the holoscreen. The chair where Grilin had been sitting was stained with blood, and we would have taken it out of there, but it was bolted into the floor.

Jini shook her head. "I'm having trouble getting the override system to let me access the messaging system. I'm going to have to use the distress signal and modify that."

"Can you do that?" I said.

"Uh, theoretically," she said. "Have I done it before? Not exactly." She swung around to another console and started typing there instead.

"The thing with Holston? I don't do things like that very often," I said. "It was really… it just happened. We tried not to, but it's… there's this instinct thing—"

"You don't have to do that," she said. "I know how lonely the resistance thing can be. More than once, I have bemoaned the lack of male sex workers for women. Why don't they have that?" She looked over her shoulder at me. "You think it's because there's no market for it or just because women don't need to pay if they're really desperate?"

I laughed softly. "Probably the latter."

"Yeah." She turned back to the console. "Still, that's a lot of work I'd rather not do. I'd really like to just order up something on my bracelet. What about you?"

I shook my head. "I mean… that sounds… what if he was a weirdo?"

"Well, it'd be pretty easy to track a serial killer who was being hired via the networks, wouldn't it? Nobody would be that dumb."

"Uh…" Yeah, I didn't know about that.

"Ha! Did it." She pumped a fist into the air.

"You did?"

"Yeah, message sent."

"Great," I said.

She tapped her fingers on the console.

"Nothing?" I said.

"It might take a while before we get a response," she said. "I was hoping maybe someone would see it right off, but... let's just give it a few hihors, huh?"

"Are you sure you sent it?"

"Positive." She got up from the console.

"I'm going to tell Holston," I said.

"Sure." She shrugged at me.

I went looking for him, but I couldn't find him anywhere on the ship. I left to go looking for him, and he came barreling out of the woods with his bolts and bow.

"What are you doing out here?" he said, wrapping an arm around my waist. "It's not safe."

"It's not safe for you either," I said. "You agreed—"

"I'm hunting," he said, dragging me back to the ship. "And I really am fine out here, so if you want to just leave me here—"

"I told you I can't," I said.

Now, we were back inside the ship.

He hesitated, looking out the open door at the outdoors.

I pressed into him. "Stay with me."

He sighed heavily. He looked into my eyes.

We kissed.

When we broke the kiss, I wordlessly entwined our fingers and led him through the corridors back to the room we'd claimed as ours.

I lay down on the bed and he climbed over me.

We kissed and kissed—hard kisses, kisses that were intent and desperate, like we both knew this was the last time and neither of us was ready for that.

But we were quiet, because we knew Jini was somewhere in the ship and that she could probably hear us.

He put his mouth on me—on my breasts, between my thighs. He made me come before he put his pleasure cock on me, and then I was twice as sensitive, and it took everything in me to swallow my moans and sighs, because he felt so, so good.

Then he was inside me again, and we were complete and connected, and I had that sensation again, of us spilling into each other as we moved together on the bed. He felt like part of me, and I felt like part of him, and I never wanted to let go of him, and I clung to him, looking up at his face, deep into his eyes, and he looked back at me, and it was the most intense, intimate thing I've ever experienced.

I came *again,* on his pleasure cock, like a star that twinkled brighter and brighter and *brighter* until I burst in a shower of starbeams and sweet glittering light. My convulsions tipped him over the edge and even our orgasms seemed to bleed into each other and everything was bliss.

He fell asleep inside me.

I fell asleep too.

I dreamed of a cabin in the woods, of the two of us walking under the stars over crunching fallen leaves, holding hands with a child with furry legs and hooves and when I looked down, I had them too. I dreamed of a donen family, and I dreamed of home and belonging, and when I woke, it was abruptly, to the sound of screams.

FIFTEEN

cypra

I was trapped under Holston's girth and weight, and I shoved at his shoulders, whispering at him to wake up.

Then I realized I was being an idiot. "Wake up!" I said, louder.

He was stirring, however, and he pushed up on his hands over me, eyes wide. "What?"

The scream again.

He tensed.

Oh, fuck, he was inside me still.

He seemed to notice this at the same time as I did. He reached between us and tugged his cock free.

I bit down on my lower lip.

We looked at each other.

Then I shoved him again. "Get off me."

He did.

I got up, finding my clothes and my blaster. I struggled into my clothes while Holston grabbed his bolts and bow. He notched a bolt into the bow and went to the door. He waited as I fastened the eazclasp of my pants and then he opened the door.

It was dark and empty in the corridor.

I brandished my blaster and nodded at him.

He eased his way out of the door and into the

corridor, covering first one way with the bow and then the other. He shook his head at me, to indicate no one was there.

I followed him into the corridor. "Let's split up," I said in a low voice.

"Can't do that, shei," he muttered. "Sorry, it's not a commentary on your ability to take care of yourself. It's just that I have an instinctive, obsessive desire to keep you safe."

"That's flattering, but—"

"It's a breeding thing, in case you're carrying my offspring," he said. "Got to perpetuate the species."

"I am not pregnant," I hissed. "And we already said that if by some chance I was, I would terminate, so you're being ridiculous."

"Not splitting up," he said.

I stalked down the corridor. Why were we *talking* about this? Someone was screaming.

He followed me.

Well, the screaming had stopped now, but that didn't mean that the danger had passed. I needed to be focusing on that, not on whatever things Holston was saying. I couldn't deny I liked that he wanted to protect me. Of course, I liked it less when he had to get all explain-y about it and say it was just because of some mythical baby I was supposedly carrying.

I refused to think about that dream.

It meant nothing.

I went slowly down the darkened corridor, clutching my blaster with both hands.

Most of the doors were shut tight, and there was nothing to see.

We came to a ladder to the upper deck, which was where the bridge was, and I wasn't sure if we should climb up there or—

I heard a noise—not a scream, but a kind of frustrated yell—coming from this way, not up the ladder, but further down this corridor, which led to the front of the ship. I started that way.

Holston thrust himself in front of me, running down the corridor with his bolts and bow, and I glared after him, annoyed, before I picked up my feet and ran too.

The corridor turned slightly, and we rounded it.

There were two donen men on the ground there, and Jini was standing over them, with a metal foot from one of the beds which she had turned into a makeshift weapon. It was dripping blood.

Both of the donen men had been stabbed with it in the throats.

They were dead.

Jini was in her pajamas and they were ripped. There was blood all over her face and her ripped clothes. She pointed her bloody weapon at us, recognized us, and then slumped into the wall.

"What the stars?" I said, pushing past Holston. "How'd they get in?"

Jini shook her head. She was trembling all over.

Holston nudged both of the corpses with his hooves. Neither moved. He looked at Jini. "Any more?"

"It was just this one," she said. "I wouldn't have been able to… if this one hadn't shown up and started fighting him, I would have…" She let out a shaking breath. "They were distracted."

He nodded. "I'll get these out of here," he said to me, gesturing to the corpses. "You take Jini to the sick bay and look her over?"

"But how did they get in?" I said.

"Okay, I'll do a perimeter check first," he said. "I'll

make sure if there are any breaches, any obvious places they've broken in, we'll know. But I need you someplace safe, got it?"

Jini shook her head. "No alarms went off. If any part of this ship was damaged because something was trying to get in, we'd have been alerted. I checked over all of that when I was doing diagnostics before I sent off the message to the resistance."

"So, what?" I said. "They had access?"

"You said people can download codes," said Holston.

"Diagnostic report," said Jini.

There was a beep, and the ship's AI voice said, "What system?"

"External access," said Jini.

"What time frame?"

"Past twenty hihors," said Jini.

The computer began spitting out every time myself or Holston had entered the ship, categorizing them as using the resistance override codes I'd been given, but then it said that less than a hihor ago, the ship had been accessed by a key scan.

Jini's eyes widened.

"Report complete," finished the ship's AI.

"Diagnostic report," said Jini again.

"What system?"

"External access, key scans only," said Jini.

"What time frame?" said the AI.

"Past two hihors, indicate to whom keys are registered."

"One key scan, Grilin Hollek," said the ship's AI.

Jini blanched.

"He's dead," I said. "He's very dead, and—"

"He said he lost it," said Jini. "We set down on the

planet, and he was acting kind of strange, and he left to go and look at the ship, he said, but when he came back, he said he lost his key, and he took mine."

"Well, they found it, then," I said, gesturing at the dead donens.

"Or he gave it to them," said Holston.

"Why would he do that?" said Jini.

"You said he locked you in a closet?" said Holston. "Stunned you?"

Jini nodded. "Yes, but why would—"

"Let's say you're in a fertility cult," said Holston. "Let's say you think that you should mate in the old way, up here during Star Season. Let's say you have no trouble convincing a bunch of donen men to join your cult."

"But I bet you don't get a lot of female volunteers," I said.

"Not so much," said Holston.

"But it's worse for men," I said. "You guys have to fight each other, and—"

"We have antlers," said Holston. "What chance did that woman we saw get gored stand against that vvoln? What chance at *all?*"

"Even so, how do you get men to volunteer for this?" I said.

Holston shook his head.

I hugged myself. "But they did seem..." The men who'd come after me, who'd tried to force themselves on me, they did seem on board with it, and they did seem like volunteers. "Men are just stupid, is that it?"

"Maybe they aren't into it at first, and then they go off their suppressants, and then..." Holston shrugged. "Then it's like all your higher-level thinking stuff is muted."

"Oh, that's *you?*" said Jini, looking at him with wide eyes.

"Don't worry," said Holston to her. "I thought I was a sociopath, but I've honed in on her and I'm not nearly as bad as I was. I won't touch you, that's for sure. I've got a vested interest in her at this point. Sunk cost, all the seed I've dumped in her. Instinctively, I'm more drawn to keeping her alive than fucking anyone else. You're good."

"You know what?" I said. "I can do without— "

"Okay, whatever with you two," said Jini. "I'm still confused. You're saying that Grilin was part of this and he brought me and Panna here to be raped by this fertility cult?"

"I think so," said Holston. "I think that's exactly what happened."

"Why'd he shoot us, then?"

"He tried to stun you and keep you captive, but when you fought back, he defended himself," said Holston.

"I guess so," said Jini.

"One of them has the key," I said. "Otherwise, how did they get in?" I went down on my knees and began hunting all over the donen for the key. But he was naked, and there was nowhere to keep a key. They weren't huge things—just scannable pieces of thin plastic, but if he had it on him, I'd see it.

"Maybe someone let them in and then kept it?" said Jini. She licked her lips. "Location of Grilin Hollek's key."

The AI answered. "Grilin Hollek's key is not aboard this ship."

"So, they have it, then," said Jini. "They still have it, and they can get onboard whenever they want."

"You're going to have to fly the ship," said Holston.

Jini rubbed her forehead. She smeared blood over where her fingers had been. "I think you're right."

"You need to get cleaned up, first," I said. "And we need to check you out on the sick bay." I turned to Holston. "You deal with the bodies?"

He nodded. "I got that, yeah."

"Let's go, Jini," I said, putting a hand on her shoulder.

* * *

holston

I took the bodies outside and buried them next to the rest of the bodies.

So many dead.

The truth was, I'd be happy to get out of here.

I looked out into the darkness, the trees hanging with dripping shadowy leaves, wondering if they were out there looking at us.

I made a rude gesture with one hand and swung it around, just in case they were.

Then I climbed back on the ship and stalked through it, following her scent, until I found Cypra. She was on the bridge with Jini. I went directly to her and pressed my body into the back of hers, winding an arm around her possessively. I stuck my nose down into the place where her shoulder met her neck and inhaled.

It was better being near her.

When we were apart, I felt a low level of panic.

Mine, I thought.

She sighed, tilting her head back, melding into me like we belonged together.

"We have a problem," said Jini.

I let go of Cypra. "Of course we do," I said. "Of course it would be too easy to just blast off into space and leave this nightmare behind." And when I flipped them all off out there, that... yeah, that had probably been a bad idea.

Jini got up. "It's, um, it's just that there's a tether."

"Oh, of course he tethered the ship," I said, letting out a little laugh.

"But how?" said Cypra. "What did he tether it to?"

Tethers were typically engaged in parking areas, a measure of security that meant that a ship couldn't take off unless it was disengaged. It usually had to be done manually, outside a ship. For a tether to work, there had to be a tether grid.

"He used the pole's magnetic pull," said Jini. "I'll just go out there and undo it."

"I'll undo it," I said. "There's no reason for you to go out there, either of you."

"I can do it," said Jini.

"I know you can," I said, "but why don't you let me do it?"

"I'll take a blaster," said Jini.

"Why didn't you have a blaster in your quarters?" said Cypra. "When you were attacked by the donen?"

"I forgot to charge it," muttered Jini. "But I got a new cartridge, and I'm good now. So, it's fine."

"And we need you to fly the ship," I said. "We don't need me for anything. So, I'll go and do it, and you two stay here and shoot anything that comes into the bridge."

Jini surveyed me. "Gotta say, I don't love your macho shit, but you do make a good point."

Which was how I ended up outside the ship wrestling with the tether in the darkness.

It should have disengaged when I went out and used the ship's tool on it. It should have, but it hadn't. No, it looked like Grilin had smashed the receptor so that the tool couldn't hook in where it was supposed to anymore, and now it was stuck tethered.

I was laboriously chipping away at the pieces of the smashed receptor to clear that away. Once I did that, I should be able to fit the tool against it and get it to disengage, but I had to clear it all off and there were a lot of pieces.

Midway into this, Jini showed up, blaster in hand, to check on what was taking me so long.

I showed her what had happened, and she offered to help, but it wasn't really a job that two people could do. There wasn't room for more fingers getting out all the slivers of smashed receptor.

She went back inside.

I went back to it.

Finally, I had them all out, and I tried the tool.

No, it wasn't connecting.

Lose me in deep space, it should connect.

I looked it over, angry—probably angrier than I should have been, which was due to the rut and the way it was affecting my emotional equilibrium.

I sucked in a deep breath and forced myself to my hooves. I made myself walk away before I decided to start kicking the tether. If I damaged it further, the tool would never fit in there.

When I was calmer, I came back and looked at it again.

Ah.

That was the problem. There was a little piece stuck down in there. I wasn't going to be able to get it with my fingers, but maybe if I turned the tool and used the edge of it?

Yeah, that was going to do it.

Just like—

Five points of bright, awful pain in my back.

I cried out, stunned, back arching, instinctively reaching behind me. I collided with flesh, and then the pressure let up, but it still hurt.

I crumpled down to my knees, but I forced myself to turn immediately. There on the ground, I glowered up from under my antlers.

It was another donen. His own antlers were red with blood. He'd had them in my back, I realized. That was what had hurt me. He sneered at me.

I fumbled for the knife I'd brought with me, strapped to my ankle. The women had tried to convince me to bring a blaster, but I'd brought this instead. Maybe that was dumb, but I figured I should use what I was familiar with, and I didn't often use a blaster.

I brandished it, pointing it at him. "Back off."

"You're going to surrender one of the women," he said. "You don't need them both."

"This some weird religious thing?" I said. "You guys out here worshiping the star spirits?"

"Fuck no, we're just getting in touch with our own actual *bodies*," he said. "It's natural to mate this way."

"It's dangerous as fuck," I said. "Sometimes the natural way isn't better."

His nostrils flared. "There have been casualties. But when the children are born in the spring, it will all be worth it. We do this for the next generation, for our sons and daughters, and—"

But he never finished that sentence, because I sprang up with my knife and stabbed him in the stomach.

He went backwards, grunting.

I tugged the blade out.

He grabbed at his wound.

"That's not necessarily going to kill you," I said, nodding at him. "But you're not in any position to mount anyone either. So, assuming you guys had some way to get up here, some transport, you get yourself out on it, back to some medcenter. When I get out of here, I'm reporting this whole crazy thing, and the authorities are going to come up here and haul you all off for rape and murder."

He clutched at his stomach, moaning. "Fuck, that hurts," he whispered. He looked at me, tears in his eyes.

I gestured with the knife.

His eyes widened. "Don't, please, don't."

"Go," I growled.

He nodded. "I'm going." He clutched his bleeding stomach and hobbled away.

I snatched the tool up off the ground and pressed it against the receptor.

The tether snapped free.

I let out a triumphant breath and hurried back onto the ship.

SIXTEEN

cypra

Liftoff was rocky.

The whole ship shook and made strange noises and Jini swore a lot in Common and Cobran and some other language, which was probably her native Abbunian language for all I knew.

But somehow we made it into orbit.

At that point, I took Holston to the sick bay to bandage him up from where he'd been skewered by that other donen's antlers. Holston still had some of that gladiator ointment, and he had me put that on him, saying it would heal up in no time.

Jini set a course for the closest spaceport and got the manifests ready for the fake ship IDs we'd been set up with by the resistance. When we were close enough, she shot that off to the tower there, asking for permission to land. They answered the query, sent us back a slot in their landing queue, and took control of the ship remotely.

Then we sat, hovering in the air, waiting for our turn to land.

Holston and I were in seats at the back of the bridge, both of us strapped in. He was holding my hand, and I was letting him.

Jini was busy sending off more communications to

the resistance, and my bracelet worked now, so I could have done that, but I didn't. I sat there, holding Holston's hand, and I looked at him a lot, looked at him in profile, trying to memorize everything about the way he looked. When he'd catch me looking at him, he'd turn to look at me.

I would immediately look away.

Finally, I said, "I thought you'd insist on staying up there."

"Nah," he said.

"I just thought it would wound your pride to not be able to hack it or something."

"It's needlessly dangerous up there," he said. "You were right."

"Yeah, it really was," I said.

"I've got to report it all to the authorities," he said. "Put a stop to it."

"Yeah, that makes sense." I nodded.

"Besides, I… you… I mean, what if you needed…"

"Needed what?"

He squeezed my hand. "I just… I don't like being separated from you."

I drew in a sharp breath. I squeezed his hand back. "I know," I whispered. "I know exactly what you mean."

And we didn't let go of each other, not the whole time we sat in the queue, not when our ship was pulled down for a landing, not when we were safe on the ground.

Jini looked at us, sitting there together, touching.

And I flinched and pulled my hand out of his hand.

And he folded his arms over his chest.

Then we both stood up.

"So, there's nothing yet from the resistance," said Jini. "But since this ship is here in this commercial spaceport, I imagine they won't contact it. We'll both probably get separate communications from our contacts via bracelet. Until then, I guess we find somewhere to hole up for the night, but it doesn't need to be together."

"I guess not," I said.

"So, uh, thanks, Cypra," said Jini.

"Yeah, of course. It was my mission." I paused. "You sure that the resistance knows where we are?"

"Positive," said Jini. "Let's get off this hunk of metal, huh?"

We followed her off the ship.

Once we were out in the spaceport, she went her way, and then Holston and I were alone, and we eyed each other.

I took a deep breath. "Um, so how far is this from your home?"

"I can get public transport," he said. "Probably a few hihors by a public speeder."

"You going to do that tonight?"

"Uh… I'm going to go report what's happening near the pole to the authorities," he said. "After that, it'll be late, so…"

"Well, you could contact my bracelet if you want," I said. "We could, um, have another night together."

He smiled. "Yeah?"

I nodded, smiling too. "Yeah."

He kissed me. His voice dropped into a lower register. "I'd like that."

I clung to him. I didn't want to let go of him.

But when we left the spaceport, he went off to talk to the local authorities, and I went to find a nearby hotel room.

I got settled in, paying for the room with credits that

were still in my account for this mission, put there by the resistance.

First thing I did was to take a real honest-to-goodness shower. I'd gotten clean on the ship, but there hadn't been water reserves, so I'd had to take one of the forced air showers, which worked, I guess. But water showers were much more pleasurable, I thought.

I let the jets of water wash over me, and then I wrapped up in the provided robe from the hotel and sprawled out on the bed.

I checked my bracelet, but I'd had no communication from Sienne yet.

I wondered if I should contact her.

Then I got a message from Holston. *This is taking longer than I thought it would.*

I had to laugh. *How long did you think it would take?*

I don't know. Not this long. They're making me wait while they call in one of the PWIs. Apparently, they've been trying to nab these guys for a while.

PWI stood for planetary-wide investigators. *Good thing you're there to help.*

I'd rather be with you.

I grinned. *I'll be here when you're done.* Then I typed in the information about the hotel and what room I was in, so that he could come straight here when he was done there.

We chatted a little longer, and then he had to go.

I made food for myself in the replicator. I figured I could make some for him when he got here. The replicator wasn't too fancy. It had a few presets, mostly simple fare. If you wanted anything better, you'd have to go down to the lobby and pay for the ones in the hotel eatery.

But Holston showed up while I was eating.

I let him in to the room and he pulled me into his arms, and I grinned up at him, giddy at the sight of him, the scent of him, the feel of him.

"I missed you like crazy," he growled in my ear, and I shivered.

We kissed and kissed.

He pulled back. "You're eating?"

"Um, I can program the replicator for you?" I gestured, giving him a grin and waggling my eyebrows.

He laughed. "Is it one of the standard ones? Like five options?"

"Mmm," I said. "Admittedly, it's not fresh meat cooked over an open flame, but it's what I'm capable of."

He kissed my forehead. "I'll do it. You finish eating."

I went back to the table where I'd been eating and he bent over the replicator and joined me in a hidosec.

"So, I told them the coordinates for the corpses that we knew about, and I reported everything that we saw. Apparently, this is not the first they've heard of this," he said. "Two women managed to get away, one last gecycle and one two gecycles before that."

"They've been doing this for gecycles?"

"Yeah," he said. "They're not a cult. Well, they are, but it's not like a spiritual thing. They think they're getting in touch with nature or something. It's this real stripped-down, back-to-the-wild thing."

"Like you?"

"Nothing like me." He gave me a withering look and he ate some of the food in his bowl. It was some kind of noodles with a brown sauce and some veggies. It must have been one of the Ohkkian meals which I hadn't recognized.

I snickered.

"Okay, I see why you would say that," he said, gesturing with his fork. "But they're on another level."

"Definitely," I said.

"Anyway, the PWIs know this because they talked to these women who got away, but the problem is that the places where the women were kept were temporary structures, like tents and things, and when they went looking for these guys, they couldn't find them. But both times, these women haven't been able to get away until after Star Season. So, this is the first time they've had a tip during the season. And they're going up there right now."

"Oh, so they're going to get them."

He nodded. "They wanted me to come along and guide them, and I said it would be too traumatic for me."

"They let you get away with that?"

"No." He winced. "So, I had to show them my, uh, mating cock had descended and that I was afraid of losing control. They were all freaked out after that."

"Like, they were afraid you were going to hurt them?"

"Just freaked in general," he said. "Although it's not as if people don't go off the suppressants to have children, so I don't know why they were being like that. Still, I guess, having the pollen in my system, being up near the pole… *then* I thought they were going to lock me up, but I convinced them I wasn't dangerous."

I smiled at him. "So, you worked really hard to get back to me."

"It was *all* I wanted," he said, groaning a little. He set down his bowl, letting his fork clatter into it, and fixed me with this *look*.

I preened into it. "I missed you, too."

He beckoned me with two fingers.

I shook my head, coy. "You're eating."

"Fuck eating," he said.

I giggled. I swear, I giggled more around this man than I did around anyone in the galaxy. "You need your strength."

"I'll eat your pussy," he said. "That's what I really want anyway. Come *here*, shei."

I got up from where I was sitting and sashayed toward the bed, giving him my back and swinging my hips. I shot a look over my shoulder. "Come and get me."

He let out a growl and pounced on me.

I fell on the bed with a squeal, him on top of me.

He drove his pelvis into the curve of my backside. He was hard.

I gasped, wriggling my hips up into him.

He kissed my neck, my shoulders. He found that spot he'd bitten the first time, which was mostly healed but still a little tender. He licked it.

I groaned.

He ran his hands over the walls of my breasts, over my waist, over my hips, the outer parts of my thighs. "You're wearing way too many clothes," he said in a gravelly voice.

"I'm wearing a *robe*," I said, snorting.

"Take it off."

I shrugged out of it.

He snatched it from me and tossed it on the floor. He lifted up my hips and pulled me up onto my hands and knees, parting my thighs. And then he licked me.

I'd never had someone go down on me this way,

upside down, and it was intriguing and delicious, the way his tongue found my clit this way, the way he licked me from there to my opening, the way he delved into me.

I liked it. I liked being in this position. It felt dirty, animalistic, like I was giving in to all my instincts and urges, and he was happy to help me, to taste me, to pleasure me.

The pleasure swirled into me, like the vastness of space, like being surrounded in velvety darkness, and I lost myself in it, taken away by the cleverness of his tongue. I felt free and easy with him, as if none of my desires were off limits, as if anything I wanted was okay. There was no shame or worry. We were just the essence of desire together, the essence of pleasure.

"Fuck me like this," I panted. "I want your cock."

"You sure, shei?" he breathed. "My pleasure cock can't get your clit like that."

"No..." I said. "I guess it can't." I giggled again. "But maybe I want to feel it somewhere else instead."

He let out a sharp breath and suddenly his fingers were *there*, gentle, circling the bud of my asshole.

I let out a whoosh of air.

"You like *that?*" He was turned on.

"I don't know," I gasped. "I never... No one has ever touched me like you're doing."

"No?" This pleased him. He brushed his fingers over my puckered opening.

I gasped again. "That's..."

"Yeah?"

"Nice." It was. It was a very sensitive place, and his fingers felt nice there, but I had to admit that his fingers gently brushing any part of my skin would probably feel nice. Was it a sexual feeling, or was it just an intimate one? I wasn't sure.

He suddenly pressed against me, his finger penetrating me.

I yelped. "No." That had *not* been nice.

He laughed. "Sorry." His finger was not there anymore. "Sorry, so sorry, shei."

"I don't want it *in* me. I just want your pleasure cock against me there, rubbing me with its little pulses, that's all. Please?"

"I can definitely do that for you," he said hoarsely.

"Mmm," I breathed.

"Here you go, shei," he whispered, and then it was there, his pleasure cock nestling between the cheeks of my ass, rubbing itself up against my opening, against the place between my pussy and my ass, and it began rippling against me immediately. "It's yours, Cypra. Both of my cocks are yours. *I'm* yours."

I let out a long, slow, deep moan of satisfaction. "My Holston," I whispered.

"Yours," he affirmed. "How's that feel, sweet girl?"

"Good," I said. It did. The surges were traveling deep into me, and I felt myself twitching and responding. I suddenly remembered that my clitoris was not just the hood, that there were internal elements of it that went all the way down into little wings around my vaginal opening, and I realized that the pleasure cock must be stimulating that part of it like this, and I moaned again. "So good, Holston, so good."

"You ready for something in your pussy, then?"

"Please?" My voice was threaded full of the pleasure I was feeling. "Fill me up, Holston."

"Whatever you need," he said in a low, affected voice, and then he was pressing inside me.

Oh, stars. That was good. Now, with his big, thick

cock inside me, the wings of my clitoris were trapped between his cocks, and it was phenomenal.

I made a mewling noise, hardly able to think because of how overwhelming that was.

"Shit, you feel amazing," he grunted. "Lose me, shei, you have the most perfect pussy of all time."

I jerked against him, liking that, liking *him*, liking *this*.

He started to thrust. Now, the swollen internal part of my clitoris was being rubbed inside by his mating cock and his pleasure cock was sending little pulses of rippling surges from the outside, and I began to shake and shudder and let out strange, mangled noises that I couldn't contain.

I was going to come, I realized.

I'd never come this way, never from this part of my clitoris, and it was the same feeling but not. It felt earthier, somehow, deeper, and I felt it building in me like a sunrise, the sky growing lighter and lighter as the brightness came for me, until the sunbeams burst through and I erupted into ecstatic convulsions, which I punctuated *very* vocally.

"Holston, *there*. Like *that*. Please. *Please*. I *need* it. Oh, stars, I'm close, I'm *close*, I'm *there*. I'm coming, I'm coming, I'm com—"

He slammed into me, cutting me off with the ferocity of his thrust, how deep it was, and then *he* was coming and we were both just sighing together, our voices needy and soft and pleased.

I collapsed on the bed.

He went with me, but gentler, so that he didn't land on me, just settled against me.

I moaned, closing my eyes.

He fitted his teeth to the place on my neck he'd

bitten before. He didn't bite down, but he gently scraped his teeth there, back and forth.

"Nap," I said in a scratchy voice.

"Mmph," he moaned.

SEVENTEEN

holston

When we woke up, we made love again.

This time, we were face to face, and it was soft and gentle, just rocking against each other, slowly easing into our pleasure, which came for us like the lap of low tide, soft waves edging us further and further until I broke.

I came before her again, so that meant I got to lick her to her climax, got to taste myself in her, something that somehow grew more and more gratifying the more I did it.

Afterward, I rolled over, careful of my antlers, and pillowed my head on her thigh to look at the ceiling. "When you go to the resistance, can I come with you?" I said.

Shit, had I said that out loud?

"What?" She shifted under me, shocked.

I didn't move, trapping her thigh. "Nothing. That was… I'm barely awake. Forget it."

It was quiet for a little while.

"You mean that?" Her voice was tiny. "That's what you want?"

"More than anything," I said in a low voice. Now, I did move. I turned over to look up at her face.

She bit down on her lower lip, furrowing her brow.

I climbed up to pull her into my arms. "Hey, I don't mean... just until I get through this, I guess. I know you have your resistance thing, and I know that's your most important thing. Maybe I'd just be in the way, but I thought maybe I could help or something."

"Get through *this?*"

"Get through my rut," I clarified.

"Oh," she said softly.

"Or..." I swallowed. "No, never mind."

"Or what?"

"I don't know," I muttered.

"Or longer? Longer than that?"

I let out a breath. "That's insane."

"It is," she said. "You live here. You love living here. You have that amazing house that's built around trees, and you can't come with me and be part of the resistance, because you don't even care about the resistance, and you don't—"

"I care about *you*, though."

A long pause. "Do you?" She sounded so hopeful, like she wanted to believe it, but couldn't.

I pushed up so that I could look into her eyes. "I'm in love with you, I think."

She let out a devastated noise.

I winced. "Shit. If I'm freaking you out, I don't mean—"

"No, I think, me too," she said, but she sounded like she was going to cry. "I'm in love with you, too, Holston."

I kissed her. "Yeah?" I was grinning. "Really?"

She cupped my face with both of her hands and forced my face back. She looked into my eyes. "You're not in love with me. It's your... it's a chemical thing."

"Oh, come on, shei. When is it *not* a chemical thing?

Isn't that what love is? No matter what species you are. How many different observations have been made in Toth labs, right?"

She considered this. "I mean... yeah. Love is about chemicals in the brain, I guess."

"Yeah," I said. "Reward chemicals, bonding chemicals, satiation chemicals, protection chemicals. It's just a cocktail of things that are firing in our synapses, but that doesn't mean that it's not real."

She nodded slowly, and her fingers on my cheeks became a caress. "Yeah..."

"I'm not saying this didn't all start because of going off my suppressants, and I know the way it started with you, the first time I had you, was—"

"It was intense," she said. "That's all."

"I know it's been a journey," I said, "but what I feel for you right now, it's more than all of that. Maybe that was the spark, but it lit a huge blaze that has taken over me, and I... I love you, and I know it's real. You feel it, too, don't you?"

She let out a helpless laugh. "Oh, stars, I do. I really do."

"Look, I'd ask you to stay with me, but you'd be miserable," I said, grinning at her. "I don't want to do that to you, so let me come with you."

"Are you serious right now?"

"Would I lie to you about this?"

She let out a noisy breath. Her eyes were shining. "It's just... it's just..."

I pulled away. "Hey, maybe it's... you keep saying that 'intense' thing, and I know you said that you didn't feel assaulted, but maybe it *is* like a trauma response, and maybe what you need is to be away from me—"

"No, Holston, you are the opposite of a sexual predator. You're a good person. You're sweet to me, and I don't… *no*."

I hesitated.

She shook her head, patting my cheek. "Don't say that ever again. You did *not* assault me, *no*."

I wanted to believe that, so… I just let myself. I let out a breath. I swallowed a lump that had somehow formed in my throat.

She stroked my eyebrow, her touch impossibly gentle and affectionate.

I shut my eyes, basking in that touch. I *was* in love with this woman, and everything about her was bliss.

"Won't *you* be miserable, though?"

"No way," I said. "The best things in life require sacrifice. I want to put you first."

Her lips parted soundlessly and she gave me this *look*…

I grinned at her. "Yes?"

"Yes," she said. "Yes, yes, *yes*."

* * *

cypra

"Um, so do you guys have room on your ship for an extra recruit?" I said quietly to the holoprojection of Sienne that was coming out of my bracelet.

Holston was still asleep.

After our declarations of love for each other, there had been even more sex, which was kind of crazy, considering how much we'd already done it. We were insatiable, though. I couldn't get enough of him.

"What are you talking about?" said Sienne.

"Not so loud!" I shushed in a whisper. I got up and took the bracelet out onto the small outdoor balcony, where it was as humid as ever. It was so gross and disgusting on this planet, seriously. What I wouldn't give for a mission to an ice planet next. I shut the door. "There. Okay. He can't hear us."

"Stars, you did it!" said Sienne. "You had sex with that donen wild-man guide!"

"I…" I let out a breath. "He… it's more than sex."

Sienne grinned. "Really?"

"Really," I said. "He said he wants to come with me. He wants to join the resistance so that we can be together."

"Like me and Caspe!" She clapped her hands. "So perfect. Yes, of course, we'll come get you both. I'm so happy for you."

I giggled. Okay, it wasn't in front of Holston, but it was because of him.

"You are *beaming*," said Sienne. "I have never seen you look so happy in all the time I've known you."

"You, um, you don't think it's fast?"

"It's always fast," said Sienne dismissively. "People say this crap all the time, like, what's that human saying? 'Fools rush in'?" She said it in English. "You've heard that?"

"Yeah," I said. "It means that only crazy people make lifetime commitments really quickly."

"But love *is* fast," she said. "You connect with someone, and there's this *jolt*, you know? And then all you want is to be around that person, like you can't bear to be separated from them?"

"Yes," I said. "Yes, exactly that."

"And I feel like the only thing that kept Caspe and me apart for very long was both of us fighting to accept it, you know?"

"I do," I said. "I mean, I'm kind of fighting it now."

"Don't," she said. "Don't, just let yourself be happy.

Come on, Cypra, you deserve this. You've been waiting long enough."

I grinned. "I really have, though."

"I am *so* happy for you."

EIGHTEEN

holston

I was lying on a small bed on a distant planet in what was a resistance outpost. I'd had to go through several layers of security to get here. They'd taken my bracelet. They'd subjected me to a full cavity search. It had been intense.

Cypra hadn't been there, because she was delivering the schematics for the ion cannon—which was the whole reason she'd gone up to that ship near Ohkk's pole in the first place—securely to her superiors in the resistance.

But right now, Cypra was lying next to me on the narrow bed, her body melded into mine.

Half a gemoon had passed since we left Ohkk. We'd spent every night together since then, on Caspe's and Sienne's ship, assisting them with a smuggling mission they'd had to complete before dropping us off here.

Well, assisting might be putting it kind of strongly, because Cypra and I had been really distracted. We'd make plans to help them do things and then be screwing when an alarm went off and ignore it when one of them queried our door and never make it out to help them after all.

That didn't happen every time, but…

The two were friendly enough, but they teased us

mercilessly, saying that we had such loud sex that we couldn't hear alarms.

I didn't know what they got up to with all of his tentacles, but I was trying not to feel, uh, inadequate. I had two appendages, which seemed like a lot until... yeah...

"I mean," I was saying, "it's up to you."

"It is not up to me," she said, lifting up her head to look at my face. "It's your body. You decide."

"I told you already my cocks belong to you," I said.

"Yeah, but they don't *really*." She glared at me.

I chuckled softly. We were discussing whether or not I should take an injection that would make my mating cock retreat into my body and make my oral suppressants work again. "They do, though," I whispered, and both of them were suddenly twitching.

She shivered against me. "Stop it. We're in the middle of a serious conversation here, Holston, and you're not going to distract me."

"Except it's fun to distract you?"

She smoothed her palm down my chest. "Later," she said, her voice decidedly throaty.

I shut my eyes, grinning happily. Leaving Ohkk, coming with her, it was the best decision I'd ever made. I'd never been this content in my entire life. She was everything. I adored her. I was just lucky she'd let me come along.

"Well, how long until it, um, retracts on its own?"

"Maybe never?" I said.

She sat up. "Your species is seasonally fertile."

"Yeah," I said. "But once my body is making this cocktail of whatever it's making, I'm in the rut until... My body is designed to keep mounting you until I, you know, accomplish fertilizing you."

She giggled. "Oh, so... your body will know that I'm pregnant?"

"I think it's more like once a donen woman is pregnant, she instinctively stops being receptive to sex, and then if a male doesn't get lucky for a while, his mating cock goes back into hibernation. Obviously, our ancestors would have the two gemoons of the Star Season and then we'd go back south, and by that point, the males were probably too exhausted to do anything and were just lucky to have survived. Not having to fuck anymore or fight off competitive males was probably a relief."

"Huh." She nodded.

"Maybe I would scent it if you were pregnant?" I said. "Maybe it would affect me. I don't know."

"Well, I guess you don't scent anything now?" She raised her eyebrows.

"Did you get your implant looked at?"

"I said I would, didn't I? Don't nag me."

"It's kind of a big deal."

"I said I would."

"So, you did?"

She nodded. "It's fine."

"Then why are you worried about me scenting anything?"

"I'm not. I was just asking."

I eyed her, feeling a little concerned about that entire exchange for some reason. Was she acting weird?

"Well, what do you want to do?" she said. "With your cock out, in the rut, you said your higher-level thinking was muted."

"Yeah, that doesn't seem as bad," I said. "I mean, I'm obviously connected enough to you that I can be in love with you, so I'm not... I don't think I'm a sociopath anymore."

"I never thought you were a sociopath," she said, laughing. "All right, regardless, I guess the most pertinent question is, do you want your mating cock out constantly?"

"I…" I shook my head. "No?"

"Okay, then, get the injection."

"But you… you won't mind?" I said. "It's just… it's in the way, and it's always getting erect at the most inopportune times, and it's not like I can't go off suppressants sometimes if we want it again, but it's kind of distracting, and I feel sex crazed."

She nodded. "Okay. That all makes sense to me."

"But I won't be able to penetrate you."

She picked up my hand and held up my fingers pointedly.

I laughed. "True, I guess…"

"To be honest, penetration is not necessary," she said. "I almost never bother doing that when I'm masturbating, and I am more than happy with your pleasure cock. You're sure it's enough for you?"

"I'm used to that," I said. "Yeah, it's definitely enough for me."

"Then I think we're both fine with it?"

I let out a breath. "You're sure?"

"Definitely." She stroked my face. "This thing with us, it's not about sex."

"No," I said, smiling at her. "I mean, the sex is nice, but it's not why I feel the way I feel about you."

"Exactly." She kissed me. "I love you."

"Lose me in deep space, I love you, too," I breathed against her lips.

She straddled me. "Let's make good use of him before he goes back to sleep?"

I chuckled, liking the way she was talking about my cock like it was somehow a separate entity from me. My mating cock hardened immediately. I shut my eyes. "You woke him up talking about him."

"Did I? Is he all stiff for me?"

I groaned. "Stiffer than stiff, shei."

"Maybe he wants me to rub him a little bit?"

"*Please.*"

She did, stroking me from root to tip, her sweet little fingers gripping me, squeezing me, making my eyes roll back in my head. "Maybe," she whispered suggestively, "he wants a kiss?"

"He *does,*" I said.

"A wet kiss?"

"A kiss with a lot of tongue," I said. "More of a sucking sort of kiss, really?"

She giggled. She only giggled like that when were in bed together, and I loved the sound of it. I got even harder. She squeezed my shaft. "Well, maybe you should ask me nicely, then."

"Will you suck my cock, shei?"

"Nicely."

"Please."

"Please what?"

"Oh..." I grunted. "Please, put your pretty mouth on me. Please lick me. Please take me as deep in your wet, perfect mouth as you can manage. *Please.*"

She bent down and licked me, her pretty wet pink tongue going from the base of me all the way to the sensitive head.

I threw back my head, panting. "Fuck."

Her mouth descended onto my cock.

I looked back, watching her, taking in the erotic sight of my cock disappearing inch by inch into her mouth, feeling the sensation of her hot, sweet mouth around me, the head of me prodding her throat. "Fuck," I said again, my voice destroyed. "That's… that's… if you want me to last at all, if you want me inside you, maybe—"

"No," she said, popping off and licking around the head of me. "I want you to come in my mouth. I want to taste you, Holston."

I groaned. "You want that?"

"Mmm, so much. Come on my tongue, come right down my throat."

It was too much. I lost it, thrusting into her mouth, even though I knew I shouldn't, but she responded enthusiastically, sucking me hard, moaning as she swallowed the head of me, as I erupted into her.

I panted, squeezing my eyes shut. "I owe you, shei," I said. "Give me a hidosec, and I'll return the favor."

She curled up into me, yawning. "It's fine. I'm tired, actually."

I sifted my fingers through her hair, yawning too. "You sure?"

"Positive," she said, snuggling close.

* * *

cypra

I was glad that Holston was getting the injection to make his mating cock retract, because my implant had sort of come out.

It had happened on Caspe's and Sienne's ship one day in the shower. I didn't know how. It was kind of itching, the spot where it was, and I scratched at it, then it just… worked its way out.

It didn't look… good.

I examined it. There were these little strands that were supposed to excrete the hormones in the implant and they were, um, well, all stiff and sort of fragile. I poked them and two of them broke off.

I should have told Holston about that, but...

To say something out loud about it would mean that I had to acknowledge that it was really happening, and I...

It sounds really stupid, but I just couldn't face it.

I couldn't even think what it probably meant.

I managed to somehow keep him from coming inside me after it came out. I distracted him with blow jobs. I told him it would make me hot if he'd jack off on my tits, and he was happy enough to oblige.

I knew it was bad, because if my implant came out, I should immediately get my period.

I didn't.

I knew I should go see someone, get a test, do something.

I knew that.

But I didn't do *anything*.

It was embarrassing, really. It was entirely, completely, totally, and in every other way irrational. It was dumb. It was irresponsible. It was not even like me. I wasn't like this. I didn't run from things. I didn't hide from stuff. I faced things head on.

I mean.

I thought I did.

Anyway, Holston got his injection, and it worked right away, within hihors. His cock was gone, and he was wandering around without pants, seemingly happy. He was in the middle of resistance training, going through things like common override codes that we all had to memorize. It was like school, and he had to drill every night.

The first night when his mating cock was gone, we

messed around and had sex with his pleasure cock.

I felt like it was… different, but I figured it was me, because I was all freaked out and hiding from my implant issues. Plus, my body was probably, um… changing.

No.

I was *not* going to think that.

The next night, I tried to initiate something, and his pleasure cock didn't really get engorged.

He stretched, next to me in the bed. "Sometimes it doesn't rise to the occasion," he said, grinning. "I can use my mouth, if you want."

"No, it's fine," I said. "I'm actually tired."

"You sure?"

I yawned pointedly, a big, fake yawn. He didn't notice that it was fake or he pretended he didn't notice. I wasn't sure which. "Totally sure."

"All right, good," he said. "We can just snuggle."

"Yeah," I said, snuggling in to him.

A fogemoon passed. We had sex a few times, and each time, it felt different, not as intense, and that sensation I'd had before with him, of the two of us feeling incredibly connected, like we were spilling into each other? I didn't really feel it.

But… I don't know. It didn't bother me, exactly. I didn't even think about it, because I was too busy trying not to think about whatever was going on with the fact that my implant had been faulty for stars knew how long.

And we both ended up being really uncomfortable sleeping together on the one narrow bed, so he started taking the top bunk, and that just seemed to make sense.

Another fogemoon passed. He was having trouble

with the training, with passing the tests. He was frustrated. He said he was good at remembering things, but not really good with memorizing strings of numbers.

I tried to help him think up little mnemonics to help jog his memory, which worked for me, but it didn't work for him.

And I started feeling sick to my stomach in the mornings.

I never threw up, but I'd wake up and go and retch over and over, trying hard to bring something up, and I *knew*…

And I still didn't say anything.

And we didn't have sex.

We didn't sleep in the same bed.

It had been a gemoon and a half since we'd left Ohkk, and I found him on his bracelet, looking at holophotos of the forests on his home planet, and I…

I should have told him.

NINETEEN

holston

I didn't understand what had happened.

It was some kind of sick joke, seriously, but my mating cock retracted and I…

It was ridiculous, after all my speeches about chemicals and real love and everything else. I didn't want it to be true, but I couldn't deny that once I was back to, well, normal, I didn't feel the same way that I used to.

Once I was out of the rut, I didn't want sex nearly as much. My desire just… went away. I didn't miss it, not exactly, but it affected things, and I had to accept now that this was just part of my biology. I was part of a species with seasonal fertility, and that was simply a fact.

The way I felt about Cypra was different, too, and I hated that.

I didn't want that to be a fact, too.

It made me ill.

It wasn't that I didn't love her anymore, but I didn't feel that crazy, obsessive desire I'd felt for her before, when I'd said I wanted to leave Ohkk and be with her. And in the wake of that, I'd had to face a bunch of things.

Like, we had nothing in common.

I liked the outdoors. I liked my home planet. I liked a simple kind of life. I liked to sleep outside. I liked feeling connected to nature, to the cycles of my planet, the soil, the sky, the trees, the animals. I missed all of that.

I felt…

It hurt.

But I had said that I wanted to put her first, and I'd upended my entire existence to be here with her. So, I wanted to make this work.

Maybe I would get over it. Eventually, I'd get through this training period, and we'd go on a mission together, and my skills would come in handy when we were planetside. We'd do all kinds of camping when we were spying on Toth or doing smuggling runs or stealing away key bits of weaponry.

This part was temporary. We'd get through it. I could do this.

For her.

Time was passing, though, and I was not getting through the training period very well. I was starting to think that I was never going to memorize all the things they wanted me to memorize, and that I was never going to get cleared for field work.

It made me frustrated, and I spent more and more of my time sullen or else staring at holophotos of Ohkk on my bracelet, looking at the woods or the animals I used to track and trap.

One night, she crawled into my lap while I was doing it and she said, "Homesick? Let me take your mind off of that," and she started kissing me.

And I felt *annoyed* that she was kissing me.

Suddenly, I knew.

My whole body went rigid as the knowledge worked

through me. I pulled away from her, and I cupped her face with one hand and I gazed into her eyes. "I don't think this is going to work, shei," I said.

Her lips parted.

My stomach turned over, but I knew it was true.

She swallowed, looking away. "Yeah," she said.

I furrowed my brow. Yeah? *That* was what she said? She wasn't even going to argue with me?

She climbed out of my lap, nodding. "We rushed into this. We've really known each other less than two gemoons, and it's insane to be, like, living together, let alone for you to be… uprooted like you are."

I sat up straight. I wanted to reach for her. I wanted to take it back. I wanted… "I thought maybe it would get better if we waited. Uh, maybe it still will? I said I would sacrifice for this, and I will. I can."

She twisted her hands together. "Should it really be like that, though? Should you have to sacrifice? Shouldn't you want to be with me?"

"I do want to be with you."

She fixed me with a look. "We don't sleep in the same bed anymore."

"It's just… the beds are really small, shei, and there's nowhere for my arm to go except under you, and then it falls asleep, and I wake up in the middle of the night with this pain shooting into my wrist—"

"I know, I…" She let out a breath. "But we don't really touch each other anymore either."

I hung my head. "I think I'm just stressed," I whispered. "Once I get through these tests—" I broke off, because I wasn't even sure if I was going to ever get through the tests. I sighed. "You know, my species is seasonally fertile, and my sex drive, it's not… when I'm on suppressants…"

"It's fine," she said. "Really, that part has been kind of a relief."

I blinked at her.

She shook her head. "Not because… I mean, I *like* having sex with you. Obviously, I do. I was just trying to, um, to kiss you."

"Maybe we should do that," I said, reaching into the folds of my fur to try to find my pleasure cock. "Sex. Maybe if we're intimate now, that's what we need. Maybe if we, uh, like we could schedule—"

"Oh, stars, seriously?" She cringed.

"No?" I said. "No, obviously, that's fucked up." I let go of my cock. I slumped on the chair.

"Look, if neither of us is bothered by the lack of sex, it's fine," she said. "We never had much sex before we met, either of us, so now, we're going back to, you know, normal."

It was exactly what I had thought.

"Yeah," I said quietly. "Normal for me is to have a much lower sex drive."

"That's fine," she said.

Except it was not fine, because… because if there was no sex, there was just us, both of us here, *me* here, where I hated everything, and there was no compensation for everything I was missing on Ohkk, and I was…

What if I grew to resent her?

I never wanted to feel that way about her.

"It's not fine, is it?" she said. "You miss your home. You miss hunting. You miss your life. You're not happy with me."

"I…" I couldn't look at her.

"It's not fair for you to have to give everything up for me," she said.

"I know, but I volunteered," I said.

"And you just said it wasn't going to work," she said. "So, I guess you're unvolunteering."

I winced. "I'm sorry, shei."

She rubbed her forehead. "No... no, don't apologize. This was all insane. We should have known better. Obviously, you have to go. Obviously, this is done."

I eyed her. She wasn't attracted to me anymore, was she? Why should she be? I was a failure and I couldn't fuck her. I didn't even have a cock anymore. She said she'd be okay with me taking that injection getting it to retract, but she was dissatisfied. And if it really was all about chemicals, if I hadn't been actually in love with her but just affected by some cocktail of brain chemistry that made me want to make a baby with her and keep her safe until she bore my offspring, then... well, I couldn't blame her. I grimaced.

She was talking again. "You know it's done. We *both* know."

I sighed. I fiddled with the tip of one of my antlers. "I guess so."

"Well—well, good." She drew herself up. "I knew it was done, too, and I was blaming it on other things, but maybe it's just... maybe we were just..." She never finished the sentence.

I watched her, trying to think of what to say to her, trying to decide how to proceed. Eventually, I said, "So, uh, what happens now?"

She went over to the lower bunk and sat down. "What do you think happens?"

"I think I leave," I said.

"Yeah," she said.

Silence fell between us, and I hated it. I missed her. She was right there, but I missed her. I wanted... I needed…

"Look, it's not you," I said in a low voice. "It's this. The resistance. This place. Everything about it is artificial and built-up. It's all metal and blinking lights, and I miss the sky and the air and the trees and I can't *breathe.*"

"Well, that's why you leave," she said. "So you can go back to all of that."

"But shei, I…" Now, it was me who couldn't finish the sentence. I got up from my chair and I went to her. I sat down next to her on the bunk bed and put my arm around her. "I do love you. It's not chemicals. Maybe it's different now, less about sex or something, but I never loved you because of sex."

She snorted, but she lay her head on my shoulder. "Why did you love me?"

"I loved you because you were brave and determined and because you were willing to take risks for the things that mattered to you."

She snuggled into me. "I loved you because you were strong and capable and confident. Because you made me feel safe and because you thrilled me in some way that I couldn't even explain. But do you notice how we're both talking in past tense?"

I cringed. "I still love you, Cypra."

"Do you really?"

I let out a long, low breath.

I was gone by the next evening, on a ship to a spaceport on Kalion where I could board another ship to Ohkk. Within three gesuns, I was back at home, in my huge, empty house, that I'd made so large for no good reason.

Why had I made this thing so big?

I couldn't be there.

I went out to that bar where I'd met her, and I got very, very drunk.

I stayed that way for a while.

* * *

cypra

Then he was gone.

Better, I told myself. *It's better this way.*

He had been miserable. I had been miserable. Our relationship was never going to work, and it was cleaner this way. It was easier this way. It was better.

With him gone, I could focus entirely on ignoring the fact that I was practically throwing up in the mornings and sometimes at other times of the day, too.

I guessed that was why I didn't care so much that he was gone?

If you'd told me a gemoon and a half ago that this relationship I was in was going to blow up in six fogemoons, I would have been devastated. I would have cried.

But…

I don't know.

It had been gradual, us drifting apart. We'd been all over each other and then we'd slowly stopped touching. The slowness had made it easier. Also, I had begun to feel really responsible for him, and I didn't like seeing him so miserable away from his forests, and anyway, I was preoccupied with the changes in my body, which made me not all that interested in sex, so what did it matter?

Finally, I had to take a pregnancy test.

I glared at it, annoyed, even though I had known it was going to be positive.

What was I going to do?

Obviously, the intelligent thing to do was to

terminate. It was the only thing that made sense.

I went and made a proper appointment to get a test and have some scans done, and they told me if I wanted to terminate, they could do it there, and it would be painless and quick and like it had never happened.

The resistance was partly built on the right of women to terminate pregnancies, because it was something the Toth had taken away. When all their women were dead and their species was dying out, the last thing the Toth wanted any pregnant woman to do was terminate.

The resistance had stepped in then, and many of the connections and avenues we used today were built on giving women the ability to end unwanted pregnancies, many of which had been forced upon them by Toth violence.

So.

I could do it.

To me, it wasn't really a question about whether or not it was life growing inside me. I believed it was. But I also believed that there was a balance. I was important to the entire galaxy doing my work here for the resistance. I had the chance to save lives, many lives, people who were suffering. I had the chance to make the *entire galaxy* a better place.

And if I sacrificed this tiny unformed life within me for that, well…?

Which was the better thing to do?

Which was more selfless?

Which was more moral?

I was keeping the baby, however.

I was choosing the baby over the whole galaxy.

I wanted it.

It didn't make sense. The resistance was the most important thing to me, after all. But maybe… maybe it was the reason I'd allowed myself to believe that things could work with Holston in the first place.

They obviously couldn't have. He and I had tried, but in the end, we were too different and we wanted different things. He had to go back to his planet, and I had to stay here.

But I guessed that I did want more. I wanted the baby. It wasn't going to be easy juggling my job and a child, but I was going to do it.

And I wasn't going to tell Holston.

Really, if I'd wanted him to know, I probably would have said something before he left.

I knew that wasn't right. He deserved to know. It was not right to hide that from him, and I knew it.

But… he left.

He wanted to go back to Ohkk. He wanted to be a hunter and to be out in the wild again with the trees and the sky. He didn't want the responsibility.

It was wrong to hide it from him.

Maybe I didn't care.

Maybe it didn't make sense.

Maybe I was allowed to be irrational right now.

Maybe…

Whatever, I had other things to think about. I had to talk to the people in the resistance about my pregnancy, and we had to discuss my level of comfortability with missions at this juncture, how and when I wanted to transition into a different position, what I could do and where I could do it.

I had vitamins to take and a *lot* of sleeping to do and an array of remedies to try to see if any of them actually settled my stomach.

I had the future to think about, all manner of baby gadgets to acquire by begging, borrowing, and buying, and I had to figure out how and where I was going to deliver, because a half-donen, half-human baby would not be the same as a human baby.

So, I didn't tell him.

And gemoons passed, and my belly swelled, and the pregnancy progressed.

One day, I had to go off planet to go see a midwife in the Balanccs system who knew about half-donen babies and could examine me and tell me what kind of birth plan I was going to need to put into place.

I needed a ride, and Caspe and Sienne were on the station, so I thought I'd ask if they could take me. But Sienne didn't respond when I sent a message to her bracelet. Instead, Caspe came and sought me out where I was working on parsing intelligence we'd intercepted from the Toth military. It was mostly drudge work, reading through transcripts, listening to recordings.

I didn't mind it, however, I was finding. It wasn't dangerous like an in-person mission, but it was really important, and I was willing to experience the tedium if it meant that I had the chance of helping the cause.

"I can take you today for your appointment," he said.

"Oh, okay," I said. "Just you?"

"Yeah, Sienne's busy with some debriefing stuff, but I can do it," he said.

"Great," I said.

Later, we were on the ship together, and I was strapped into the bridge for takeoff, but we'd cleared that and we were now in space, course set, and he was unstrapping and stretching out his tentacles.

I unstrapped too. "Um, Sienne couldn't tell me that

she was busy herself?"

He glanced at me. "You noticed that she's avoiding you. She said you would. I said you wouldn't. She was right." He was tall and bald and black, his tentacles squirming around, and he wore a navpatch over one eye, a tool that space pirates used to hack navigational systems on ships. He would have been intimidating, but I knew him now, and he wasn't the least bit intimidating.

"She's avoiding me?" I was hurt.

"It's because she heard you were pregnant," he said. "She, um, she…" He shook his head. "I think she's jealous."

I drew back. "Oh. I didn't know you guys were, like, trying?"

"We are not," he said, and then he swept out of the bridge, leaving me alone and confused.

I got up and followed him out.

But he wasn't anywhere in sight.

I moved through the ship until I found him in a room that was set up like an office. He had a desk in there and he was seated at it, squinting at a holoscreen.

He looked up at me. "You want to keep talking about Sienne, don't you?"

"Well, that's really confusing," I said.

"Yeah." He nodded. "I think it's her passive-aggressive way of telling me she wants babies *now*, right? But when I ask her point blank about it? She's always like, 'Not yet.'"

"Did she say she was jealous?"

"No, not in, like, words," he said.

"So, why do you think that?"

"She said, uh… 'Oh, of course she ends up pregnant, even after that bastard Holston abandoned her. She probably doesn't even want to be pregnant, and of course *she* got pregnant.'"

I furrowed my brow. "That's not even... Holston doesn't *know*."

"Oh," said Caspe in a voice that indicated exactly what he thought of that.

I folded my arms over my chest. "I don't have to tell him."

"I think he probably wants to know," said Caspe, folding his arms over his chest, too, even as he tilted back in the chair at his desk.

"We're talking about Sienne," I said.

He snorted. "Nothing more to say about that. We're having the most polite huge fucking fight ever. I don't even know what it's about, but it's something to do with babies, and everything I say is wrong."

"Polite fight?"

"Oh, yeah, we're not yelling at each other or anything, and everything's *fine*, except she's really mad at me, and I can tell."

"Do you want to have babies?"

"I mean, the thought terrifies me," he said. "But, uh, yeah. Anything worth doing is terrifying, I figure, right? And Sienne? She'd be an amazing mother, and make up for all the mistakes I'm going to make. And... and... yeah." He gave me a shy little grin. "Yeah."

"So, you've told her this."

"I have," he said. "And she says, 'Not yet.'"

I nodded. "Okay."

"But then she gets like this when people are pregnant. You're not the first person she's been odd about." He sighed heavily. "Anyway, try not to take it personally."

I shook my head. "Well, I can try, but it's a little bit

difficult."

"So, why didn't you tell him? He seemed like a good guy. He seemed *really* into you. You guys barely came up for air when you were with us on that smuggling thing. You were constantly touching, and—"

"Shut up, Caspe."

He rubbed the back of his neck. "Oh, stars, is he, like, a jerk? Did he hit you or something?"

"*No.*"

"Oh, good," he said. "Good, that's really good."

"I don't want to talk about this."

"Yeah, I didn't want to talk about the thing with Sienne. Too bad. Why didn't you tell him?"

"He didn't want to be here. He didn't want to be part of the resistance. He has his own whole life. I don't need to intrude on that."

"Well, uh, he's clearly intruding on *your* life, what with his child growing inside you and all."

"It's *my* child."

"Yeah." He nodded. "It is. Still, Holston should know. If I had knocked up some woman, and she never told me... what are you going to do when the baby grows up and asks about his dad? Kid's going to have antlers or something, and what are you going to say?"

"The baby is a girl," I informed him. "No antlers."

"Whatever. Even if *she* looks entirely human, she's going to care about her father."

"Lots of children grow up with single mothers, and they're fine."

"If I had baby somewhere, and his mother didn't tell me, and I found out that I had missed all of the moments at the beginning—the first steps and the first words and the—"

"Stop it."

"I'm just saying, that would suck."

"Holston left, okay?"

"So, you're going to punish your unborn child because his father broke your heart?"

"He didn't break my heart. I didn't care that he left."

Caspe raised his eyebrows.

"I didn't!" I sighed. "Look, it was... you know how at the beginning of a relationship, you can't keep your hands off each other, and then, after a while, that just kind of fades out?"

Caspe coughed. "Uh...."

"Fuck you," I said, glowering at him.

"But, no, I hear that's common," he said, nodding. "I think most couples, uh, that—"

"I hate you," I decided. "I hate you and Sienne both."

He grinned, letting out a little laugh. "So, you were hot and heavy and then not?"

"It was like, *all* we were was hot and heavy," I said. "There was nothing else. We don't have anything in common."

"Well, me and Sienne, we were archenemies," he said. He considered. "Actually, I guess that just meant that we'd both been obsessed with each other for a really long time before we started fucking. And I guess we have a lot in common, because we both have experience being the admii on ships and we know all the lingo, and we've both done a lot of scavenging and smuggling jobs and we both—"

"Seriously?" I said.

"Yeah, I guess what I'm saying is that I don't understand at all and can't relate to any of your relationship problems." He shrugged.

I threw up my hands and stalked out of his office.

He used his tentacles to pull himself through the doorway just before the doors snapped closed. "Wait, where are you going?"

"I don't know," I said, turning and starting to walk down the hallway. "Look, he would have stayed if I'd told him, and it wasn't working with us. We have *nothing* in common."

"I get that," said Caspe. "But this is just why you guys broke up, right? Not why you're hiding his own child's existence from him."

"So, on Ohkk, his whole life revolved around being this, I don't know, wild man. He spent more than half of his time on these long hunting trips where he wouldn't take anything with him except a bolts and bow and he'd make his own shelter and kill all his own food and live off the land, right? That was his *thing*. And he gave that up to come join the resistance and be with me."

"But he didn't give it up. He's back there now."

"I know, but it was a big thing, this sacrifice. He talked about 'putting me first.' And if I'd told him, he wouldn't have left. And if I told him now, he might..."

"Might what?"

"Might try to come back," I said softly. "But for the wrong reasons. And I don't want to do that to him. I don't want to make him feel like he has to give everything up."

"Well, he's going to have to make sacrifices if he wants to be a dad," said Caspe. "If you don't think he's capable of it—"

"Obviously, he's capable of it. He gave up everything for me."

"Except not really, because he didn't stay."

I considered that. Caspe was right. He hadn't given

up everything, had he?

But then, I hadn't either. I wasn't willing to give up the resistance. I'd made compromises, but I couldn't let it all go.

"You don't have to be in a relationship with this guy for him to be a father to his child, you know that, right?"

I glared at Caspe. "Obviously, I know that."

But maybe I'd been thinking about all of it too narrowly. Holston had left. It was best for both of us. But I did need to think about what was best for our baby. And maybe Holston did need to know.

TWENTY

holston

I was hungover when I got the query on my bracelet from her.

Six gemoons had passed, and you would have thought I would have been over it by now. I should have been over it.

I just…

Everything suddenly seemed meaningless. I tried to get back into the things that I had done before, but they didn't feel the same. I would go out into the woods, and I would hunt or make shelter or build a fire, and I was good at all those things, but they were *empty* now, in some way they'd never been before.

So, it had become something I only did enough to make enough income to pay my bills. I did the bare minimum. It was a job, not a lifestyle anymore.

The shittiest thing about it was how much I missed it.

But when I tried to do it, it just… it wasn't enough anymore, somehow.

I knew I also missed her.

I also knew, deep down, that I couldn't have stayed there with her, that I wanted her, but that she wouldn't be enough either. I wished I could somehow have both. I thought if she was here, if I was coming home from a hunt to knowing that she was in this huge house, waiting for me, that it would make all the difference.

But what would she do here?

She couldn't just sit around in my house waiting for me all the time. That was no kind of life for her.

So.

It was what it was.

I kept telling myself it would pass, that eventually, I would feel better again, and I waited and waited, and…

I drank a *lot*.

So, there she was, a holographic image of her head and shoulders coming up out of my bracelet, and I was rubbing my face, wondering if my hair was sticking up on one side, staring at her bleary-eyed.

"Cypra," I said.

"I just have a question for you," she said.

I blinked at her. "It's been a really long time." She looked good. Her face seemed fuller, her cheeks a little rounder, and it made her seem pretty and luminous, and I remembered the way she smelled and the way she felt in my arms, and that feeling burrowed into my chest and bloomed in a bright ache.

"You're happier now, right?"

"Uh…" I ran my fingers over my hair, trying to tell whether or not it looked positively horrible. "This is the reason you contacted me?"

"I'm pregnant."

I felt as if the entire room squeezed in on me, the walls closing in, the ceiling falling on my head. I couldn't breathe.

"Did you hear me?" she said.

I choked, trying to suck in air to speak to her. "You're *what?*"

Suddenly, the holoprojected image of her pulled

back, and there she was, there was her rounded belly, and she was *really* pregnant, so that was... exactly the right time for... I made a wheezing noise, gaping at her.

"Holston?"

"Fuck," I said.

"That's what you have to say?"

"It's mine?" I said in a tiny voice.

"No, I'm contacting you to tell you that some other man knocked me up!" She was sarcastic and angry.

I winced. I rubbed my forehead, trying to gather my thoughts.

Her image changed back to just her head and shoulders.

I reached up to find my antlers, rubbing my forefinger over the tip of one. "Uh, you've known this a while."

"Yeah, I guess you're probably mad about that."

"You said your implant—"

"I know, I should have told you then, because it fell out—"

"It fell *out?*"

"I was pregnant already by then," she said. "I was kind of in denial about it for a long time—"

"You knew when I left," I said in a low voice. "You let me go and you knew."

She didn't say anything.

I could have been angry about this, but I wasn't. I only felt hurt. The ache in me opened up into a gaping well of pain. When I spoke, my voice was scratchy. "You, uh, you thought I wouldn't want it? Fuck, when I said that thing about terminating, I didn't mean I'd try to *make* you do that."

"No, no, I never thought *that.*"

"I would never tell you what to do with your own

body, shei, I would never—"

"Holston, I know that."

"Okay, so why didn't you tell me, then?" She was *pregnant*. Fuck.

"I guess I didn't want to bother you," she said.

I scratched my jaw. I was very confused right now. "Bother me? You're pregnant."

"I know that."

"So, *you're* bothered. How would it bother *me?*"

"I guess I thought... you had volunteered to leave everything behind to have a relationship with me, and then I'm pregnant," she said. "I thought you'd do it again. And I didn't want to be the person who made you give up the things you care about, not when we had already seen that it wouldn't work."

"You wanted me to stay," I whispered.

"No!"

"No?" I sat up straighter. "So you don't want me to come back now?" I could do that. I'd spent gemoons missing her, after all. This was a sign. I wasn't happy on Ohkk, not anymore. I'd probably be unhappy with the resistance, but I'd be with her, and we'd have a child together, and that sounded—

"No."

I licked my lips. "Shei, if you'd told me, I would have been there."

"I don't *want* you here," she snapped.

I flinched, like she'd open-palm-slapped me.

She sighed, massaging the bridge of her nose. "I only mean that we know it doesn't work with us. We don't need to try to get back together for the baby. When does that *ever* work?"

She was right. We weren't together. We were on opposite sides of the galaxy. If I'd really wanted to fight for her, I could have, and I gave up on her pretty quickly, all things considered.

I'd spent gemoons missing her, yeah, but I'd never tried to get in touch with her. I'd never made any attempts to get back with her.

Why was that?

Because I didn't want to go back to the resistance. That sounded like torture to me. I wanted her, but there was no way I could have her.

And now, she was going to have a baby. My baby. And I wasn't even going to be there. My face twisted.

"Holston?" she said.

I held up a hand. "Give me a hidosec," I said thickly.

"Look, I'm sorry I said that I didn't want you here, but—"

"No, no, I'm not..." I wiped my eye with the heel of my hand. "That's not why I'm like this. You're right. I was miserable there. I wanted to put you first, but, like, I *couldn't*. If I'd wanted you back, I could have tried to get you back, and I didn't."

She nodded. "Yeah," she said softly.

"But now I'm going to be a dad except... except *not*."

"No, that's why I told you," she said. "I figured you deserved to know. And if you want to be part of it, then..."

"Then what?"

"Well, we'll... we'll work it out somehow."

"Like visitations or something," I said in realization. "I get him for a couple fogemoons every gecycle? Like that?" I swallowed. "Yeah, I guess it's better than nothing."

"I'm so sorry, Holston," she whispered.

"What are you apologizing for? *I* should apologize. I'm the one who... I fucked up your whole life."

"No," she said, shaking her head. "No, I want the baby." She paused. "It's weird, right? Before all of this, the resistance was enough, but now... I need *more,* and the baby, it's... I'm ready for this."

I was not ready for this. Not at all.

"You, um, I have scans and holopics at various levels of development and recordings of her heartbeat—it's a girl, by the way—and you can see her little hooves, and—do you want to see them?"

"Fuck," I said, reeling. "A girl?"

"Uh huh."

"Yeah, I want that. *Yes.* Um, please."

"Okay," she said. "We'll stay in touch. We *will* figure this out."

* * *

cypra

I got out my bracelet and pulled up a holoprojection of myself, looking myself over, fiddling with the collar of my shirt. It was only the tenth time I'd done it.

I was being stupid.

It didn't matter how I looked.

Besides, I was huge. I was eight gemoons pregnant, and I was not remotely attractive. So, no matter what, Holston was not going to think I looked good or anything.

We were meeting here at an appointment with the midwife I was seeing. It had been a bit of a trek for him to leave Ohkk, but he had been eager to do it, saying he definitely wanted to see the holoscan of the baby live, and that he wanted to see me.

We'd been in touch fairly often, but we only ever talked about the baby. I sometimes thought I wouldn't be able to reach him, because he'd be out on a hunt, somewhere there was no network reception on his bracelet, but he never seemed to be. I tried to ask him about that, but he always brushed it aside as if he didn't want to talk about it.

Now, we'd see each other for the first time in gemoons.

I was nervous.

I couldn't help it.

My bracelet beeped, interrupting the image of myself with a message from Holston. *I'm here, coming in the front door.*

I slammed down my reflection, standing up.

Oh. There he was.

He looked around and then saw me and his face dissolved into a big grin.

I smiled back, giving him a little wave.

He hurried over to me. He started to touch me, to hug me, and then he caught himself. He let out a chuckle and shifted on his hooves. "Sorry, shei."

"We..." My voice came out shy. I peered up at him, biting my lower lip. "We can hug."

"Yeah?"

I nodded.

His arm wound around me, and somehow, even though I was the size of a planet, he made me feel small in his strong arms, against his broad shoulders. I breathed in the scent of him, and he smelled...

Fuck, how did he smell like coming home in some strange way?

I pulled away, looking up at him, a surge of turmoil rushing through me.

He kissed my forehead. "You look amazing."

Something inside me turned over, sending thrills through my body.

"Sorry," he said again. "You said hug. I shouldn't

have—"

"You look good too," I said.

He laughed. "I still have this beer belly." He touched his stomach.

I furrowed my brow. He had gained a little weight, but I kind of liked it on his frame. It made him seem softer, and anyway, I was obviously huge, so... "You've been drinking a lot?"

He shrugged. "Drowning my sorrows, whatever. I'm shaped up, I swear. I'm not going to be a drunken dad." He squared his shoulders. "Seriously, I want to be ready for this, too, like you are. I'm..." He drew in a breath and nodded.

"Drowning your sorrows?" I said softly. "You don't mean..." I touched my chest. "Me?"

"No," he said, shaking his head. "No, did I say that out loud? No, it's, you know, some totally unrelated heartbreak thing—shit. How was your trip? You get here okay?"

"Holston," I said, tilting my head to look at him. He was drinking me away? Really?

He gave me a look. "Stop it. I'm really embarrassed right now. Maybe I should go find us, like, coffee or something? Can you drink coffee when you're pregnant?"

"You said you were happy," I said.

"Did I say that?" He wouldn't meet my gaze.

Maybe he hadn't said that. "You said you could have fought to get me back, and you didn't."

"Shei..." He sighed.

"Because you thought it was hopeless? You thought I didn't want you back? You thought—"

"It *is* hopeless, isn't it?" he whispered. "We have nothing in common. We don't want to live in the same places. We can't..."

I nodded. "No, you're right." I blew out air. "You're right, obviously."

"Coffee," he said. "I think there's like a little coffee stand outside, and I'm just going to... unless you can't have it when you're pregnant."

"I can at this point," I said. "I'm far enough along, but it's so acidic that it gives me heartburn, so..."

"Oh. Right. Sorry about that. Are you, like, really uncomfortable?"

"I'm fine." I was *extremely* uncomfortable. "You should get some for yourself, though."

"I don't really like coffee. It's such a Toth thing."

"It's a human thing," I said. "The Toth stole it from..."

"Right." He nodded. "Yeah, actually, I knew that."

We were quiet.

"Uh," he said, "how long until the appointment? I thought it was soon."

"Oh, they're running behind," I said. "So, it might be an extra few hidosecs." I gestured. "We could sit?"

"Yeah."

We sat.

"Heartbreak," I whispered.

"Shei," he muttered.

It made me want to cry. Everything made me want to cry these days, of course, but... I bowed my head.

"Look, it's not that dramatic," he said. "I just would get stuck in this loop, this thought loop? Like, I *hated* it on that resistance outpost."

"I know you did."

"I wanted to come home to Ohkk. That's why I said it wasn't going to work," he said. "And then I got home, and..."

"And what?"

"It wasn't the same. Hunting, it used to mean something, and it didn't anymore. Everything felt empty. Everything felt pointless without you."

"Pointless?" I breathed.

"So, I would think that I needed you, but that I couldn't be with you, and then I'd feel like, no matter what I did, I'd be unhappy, and... so, I'd just want to shut that up, and I couldn't shut it up, so I'd get drunk." He shrugged. "It's stupid."

I wasn't sure what to say. I regarded him. "But you said you're not drinking anymore, though, so... is it better now?"

He tilted his head. "You know, it is." He rubbed his chin, considering. "I think it's the baby."

I put my hand to the curve of my belly. "The baby makes you feel as though things are less meaningless?"

"Yeah, something important to do," he said. "Make sure I'm worthy of her, make sure I can be what she needs. It's... focusing."

I moved my hand to his shaggy forearm. "I'm sorry I couldn't be that for you."

He looked deep into my eyes. "Maybe we're just not those kinds of people, shei."

"The kinds of people that love is enough for, you mean?" I said.

He nodded, looking away.

I put my hand back on my belly.

TWENTY-ONE

holston

The appointment was insane. I was awed by the sight of the holoprojection of my daughter growing inside Cypra. She was definitely half-donen. She had little itty bitty hooves and she was… was *beautiful.*

It made me feel somehow really small and really big all at the same time? Like I made that? She was half of me? Wow.

But also… how had I *made* that? How could I be a *father?* I wasn't even remotely deserving of this tiny, perfect little being and I didn't know if I could handle the responsibility of protecting her.

They gave me a holorecording of it, so I could pull it up on my bracelet and look at her. I could show her to other people. *That's my baby, right there.* It was unbelievable.

I looked up from the holoprojection at one point, to look at Cypra, and she was looking at me, instead of at the baby. Our eyes met, and she held my gaze and gave me this silly sort of grin, and it… all the feelings I'd ever had for her rushed into me as if I was being engulfed in an avalanche from behind, and I had never loved anything the way I loved in that moment.

I loved her.

I loved the baby.

I loved all of us together.

And then—

Pain.

Right on the heels of that because of the situation.

So, when the appointment was over, I tried to get away, but Cypra got a message from the resistance person who was supposed to be her ride that they were having issues getting airborne and were stuck on another planet in the system.

She told me to go, saying that she'd be fine.

"How long do you think you're going to be stuck here?" I said.

She shrugged. "Not sure. But if it becomes an issue, I can get a ticket on a public ship or something."

"Well, where are you trying to get to?"

"Same place," she said.

The resistance outpost, then. "There's no public transportation going there."

She shrugged. "I'll get close, and then someone else can pick me up."

"How long will that take?" I said.

"Look, it's all up in the air, Holston. That's how it is with my—"

"Come back with me," I said, on impulse. "Someone can pick you up from Ohkk just as easily as anywhere else."

She gave me a look. "Now you're ordering me around."

"You been eating replicator shit all this time? You're pregnant. You need real protein, okay? Not that bland stuff that's in a replicator. And vitamins. I have fruit trees in my back yard, and—"

"Holston, seriously?"

"Sorry," I muttered. I made a fist and studied my

knuckles. "Okay, I'll stay here then, just until someone picks you up."

"I don't need you to do that."

I lifted my gaze to hers. "Right." I squared my shoulders. "Right, you don't need me. I mean, you don't need me for any of this, do you?" I turned away. "Maybe it would have been better if you just never told me." Then I regretted that. I winced hard.

"You don't have to be part of it at all if you—"

"That was fucked up to say." I turned back to her. "I should never have said that shit. That was really fucked up." I hung my head.

She groaned. "Of course, you're *trying* to be part of it, and I'm not letting you, am I?"

"You have every right to set boundaries and keep me at arms' length, shei. You run the show. I won't complain. I won't order you around. I'll... fuck." I took a deep breath. "You know what? I'm going to go. And if you decide that you need anything that I can help with, you know how to get in touch with me."

"Holston..."

I winced yet again. "You want to hug goodbye or just, uh, shake hands, or...?" I really had no intention of leaving the planet. I wasn't going to stalk her or whatever. I was going to maybe, uh, track her. Watch her. Watch *over* her.

"If I come back to stay at your house, it's just a, um, platonic thing? Like, we're friends who are having a child together, right? You're not going to try to convince me to stay there longterm with you or something?"

"What?" I shook my head. "No, no way. No, this is... we tried this. It didn't work."

"Okay," she said. "Okay, actually, that sounds very

nice. I am way too pregnant to be sitting around waiting for someone to come and get me, actually."

"Okay, good," I said, grinning at her.

We boarded a transport together and I might have paid extra to get us into the bigger seats in the front of the ship, and she must have noticed, but she didn't say anything.

The trip was quick enough. We were on the side of the Ohker system that didn't have to go around the asteroid belt to land, so we were on solid ground within hihors.

We got off the ship and I took her to my speeder.

"Oh, you got it back."

"Yeah, it was just sitting out there," I said.

"Obviously, you fixed the tire."

"All new tires," I said. "Can you climb this? I really didn't think about how, uh, difficult this would be for you, I have to say."

"Yeah, I'll be fine," she said, but midway up, she looked down sheepishly at me. "Um... I'm kind of... top heavy and off balance, and—"

"I got you," I said, and I scampered up the ladder behind her and got her up into the speeder. When we got to my place, I brought over a hydraulic platform I had and lowered her to the ground that way.

She giggled when I pulled her off of it. "Oh, stars, the hardest thing about being pregnant has been accepting my limitations, realizing I need help, that I can't do everything on my own. It's the worst."

"Yeah," I said, thinking of what that would be like. "I can see that. I probably haven't been really sensitive to that, huh?"

"No, you're..." She sighed. "The truth is, most people just assume I can handle it all, and it's probably because I keep insisting I can. It's kind of nice to have someone want to take care of me a little."

"A lot," I said. "Let me take care of you a lot?" Then I put up both my hands. "No, you know what? Never mind. I didn't mean—"

"Okay," she said, and she collapsed into me, putting her face against my chest. "Okay, please. I'm exhausted."

It seemed natural to put my arms around her then, and I did.

We walked, arm in arm, her leaning against me, into my house, and I got her set up on a couch, fetching pillows for her when she told me that she could not have *enough* pillows these days, and helping her tuck them various places—behind her back, under her legs, around her pelvis.

She lay back, eyes close, moaning. "Okay, now I think I'll be comfortable for exactly two whole minutes before she wakes up and starts kicking me."

"Two minutes, huh?"

"I'm exaggerating." She sighed. "Not that much, though."

"Is there anything I can do?"

"You said you were going to feed us." She put her hand on her belly gazing up at me with half-lidded eyes. "Real protein, you said?"

I grinned. "Yeah, I can do that."

"I've been craving meat," she said, shutting her eyes.

Feed *us*. That made something rise in me, something almost primal, and I didn't know what to do with it.

Mine, said a voice inside me, a voice I hadn't heard since I'd been in the rut.

Not yours, I countered, while I cooked. I had a freezer and cooler stocked full of meat that I'd hunted, and it was easy enough to make something for her. I put together a meal of fresh food, all of it right from the actual ground, none of it processed sludge from a replicator.

I started to set the table in my dining room and then thought maybe she'd rather stay on her pillows.

When I went in to ask her, she was asleep.

I wasn't going to wake her for the world, but she suddenly clutched her stomach and let out a grunt and her eyes opened. "*Ouch.*"

"You okay?" I said.

She reached up and grabbed my hand and put it on her belly.

And there it was, a little fluttery feeling of movement under my fingers, and my heart expanded, and I felt my throat constrict, and I gasped.

Cypra pulled my face down and kissed me.

I kissed her back.

And then I pulled away. "Hey, you said…"

"I know," she said, shaking her head, looking confused and freaked out. "I don't know what that was."

"You were half asleep," I said. "You can't be blamed for whatever you did. Let's pretend it didn't happen."

"Sounds good." She grinned at me. "Does that amazing smell mean dinner is ready?" She sat up, sniffing.

"Yeah," I said. "I didn't know if you wanted to eat here or at the table?"

"Table, definitely table. Upright esophagus means less heartburn. Help me up." She held up both of her hands.

I took her hands and pulled her to her feet, and she collapsed into me again.

And somehow, she was in my arms, and somehow, we were kissing again.

When we stopped, we both just looked at each other with chagrined looks on our faces, and neither of us said anything about it.

At dinner, she moaned sexual noises about all of the food, and my pleasure cock liked it, and I sat there, watching her, glad of the table in the way to hide my obvious arousal. She ate everything in sight, voracious, and then declared there was definitely heartburn in her future, and I got up to go to the kitchen and get some willn root, which I thought she could chew and it might soothe her stomach.

I was telling her about it, and I realized her eyes were really wide, and that was when I remembered that my pleasure cock was…

I felt heat rush to my face. I wrangled it back into my fur and went to the kitchen. I came back with the root and handed it over to her.

She popped it into her mouth and chewed.

It was quiet.

"This is like… really soothing and kind of… cold?" she said. "I mean, it's not temperature cold, but it feels cold?"

"Yeah, it's been used medicinally on Ohhk for generations," I said. "It's good stuff."

"You don't find me attractive like this," she said. "Not like sexually attractive."

"Uh…"

"I mean, why was your pleasure cock…?"

"I'm really sorry about that," I said, not looking at her. "You made it very clear to me, and I… no excuses. Not proud of that."

"I'm huge," she said.

"Uh, you're... not." I shifted uncomfortably on my chair. "I mean you're *you*, and you look really good and I mean, *I* did that to you, so it makes me..." *Shut up, Holston.*

"It makes you what?" She leaned across the table, a slow smile stealing across her face.

I shook my head at her. My mouth was dry.

Her voice went low and lilting. "You want to pretend again, Holston?"

I think that's a terrible idea. "Pretend what?" My voice was hoarse.

"Pretend it's not hopeless. Pretend I could stay here and I'd actually be happy. Pretend we could make this work. Pretend we're together. That we're in love."

I let out a breath. "Oh, shei."

"We could say it," she said, reaching across the table for me. "I love you."

I shut my eyes.

Her fingers brushed mine. "Now, you," she breathed.

"I love you, Cypra," I murmured.

"Take me to bed, Holston."

"But you made me promise—"

"It's just pretend."

"But you're going to regret this, and I'm not going to be the guy who didn't respect your decision, and—"

"Pretend."

"I'm going to be strong and resist you this time," I said, opening my eyes to glare at her.

She raised her eyebrows. "Really? That's what you're going to do?"

We ended up in my bed.

She took off all her clothes, and I thought her body was the most intriguing thing I'd ever seen, and I put my mouth all over her belly and then between her thighs and she shuddered against me and let out these broken cries, and I told her that seeing her this pregnant, knowing that I'd *made her* pregnant, it made me crazy hot in a way I couldn't even fathom, and she bucked her hips up into my mouth and I licked her until she came.

Then I put my pleasure cock there, and *I* came, my pleasure cock seizing up just from the touch of her wetness, just from being between her thighs again.

But we kept going, and I made her fall apart again, and then I went off to find her as many pillows as I could so that she could be comfortable and sleep next to me, and we lay like that, peering at each other over the mound of pillows, and she kept saying it.

"I love you." She traced my face with her fingers. She touched my antlers and it made me shudder.

I said it back. "I love you, too," I breathed. "And I love the baby, and I love having you here, next to me. I love all of this." I had a feeling that when she left again, my heart was going to shatter, but every time I thought that, I pushed the thought away. I didn't need that right now.

We said it again and again, until we drifted, enfolded in the soft darkness of sleep.

TWENTY-TWO

cypra

I screamed, because there was someone in Holston's kitchen.

The person was a donen woman, and she was wearing an official-looking gleaming badge hanging around her neck, and she drew back, taking me in, and her lips parted.

Oh, stars.

You know, Holston had said a thing about an unrelated heartbreak. I'd thought he'd been deflecting, but maybe he *had* had a fling with this woman or something? Why else was she in his house?

She was gazing at my very pregnant belly. "Lose me in deep space," she said, pointing at me. "Is that Holston's?"

I put both of my hands over my belly. "Um, are you his girlfriend, because he didn't mention anything—"

"No," she said. "No, I am..." She cleared her throat, lifting a finger. "But, you know, he definitely didn't say anything to me about some pregnant human woman either." She spread her hands and talked directly to my belly. "But it lines up, look how far along you are, and he was in a rut, and he disappeared and practically blew the entire case when we needed his testimony, and—" She broke off. "Fuck." She went around me and out of the kitchen.

I followed her. Holston's house had a lot of windows and it was made out of a lot of wood and natural finishes. There were a lot of plants inside, hanging in baskets, sitting on the floor in pots. It was nice.

I mean, I loved his house. I had loved it the first time I came here. It was a *really* great house.

"Look, he probably didn't tell you because he didn't know," I said, defending Holston for some stupid reason. Of course, I was still confused. She *wasn't* his girlfriend? "I didn't tell him until recently, and he made it out like he wasn't involved with anyone, but then I guess I didn't act like I wanted us to be romantically involved at all, so..." I did keep saying that we were just pretending last night, which we were, but... but I'd had this stupid idea when I woke up this morning, and now he had a girlfriend, and that was still cheating, even if it was pretend, and I was not going to be the other woman, no way.

"He and I are not involved," she said, going straight for a small wooden table where there was a handwritten note. She snatched it up, letting out a relieved breath.

"Natta?" said a voice from the doorway.

Both me and the donen woman turned.

Holston was there. "Natta, what are you doing here? Is there some new development with the case, because I thought we were just waiting for sentencing? Did you let yourself into my house?"

The donen woman—who must be Natta—cringed at him. "This was a huge mistake. I am mortified, and I'm leaving. Forget I was here."

"So, it's not about the case?"

"What case?" I said.

"Uh, Natta here is PWI. She was the lead investigator on the case with the crazy guys at the pole, who were capturing women and raping them?"

"Oh, right," I said. "There was a case."

"Yeah, I testified," he said, scratching the back of his head. "I did a lot of one-on-one work with Natta."

"Oh," I said in a different voice, looking her over.

"No," she said. "Not like that." She sighed. "I'm leaving."

Holston furrowed his brow. "So, why are you here?"

"It's... can we pretend I'm not?" said Natta with a too-wide smile. "I'll go, and you two can..." She gestured. "Have a baby together."

"Well, she's having a baby," he said. "We're not really..." He glanced at me. His jaw worked. Then he noticed the note Natta was clutching to her chest. "What's that?"

"This?" She looked at it, and she crumpled it up. "Nothing. Nothing at all."

"Wait, were you...?" He drew back. "Was it like... was it like an I-like-you note?"

"Goodbye," said Natta, pushing past him, shoving him into the hallway to get past him.

He let her. He collapsed into the wall and stood there, blinking, looking shell shocked.

She rounded a bend in the hallway, went out of sight, and then I heard the door to the house shutting in the distance.

I looked down at my feet, clasping my hands together.

Holston peered into her wake. "I maybe was oblivious to that. She was kind of... now that I think about it, I should have noticed, but I was just so..." He looked back at me. "I mean, *you*."

I lifted a shoulder. "You want to go after her?"

His eyes widened. "Is that what you want me to do? You want me to go after another woman the morning after you and I…? While I still smell like you? Is that what this pretending thing is?"

I looked away, a lump rising in my throat. I shook my head. "No. No, I don't want you to do that at all."

He let out a harsh laugh. "Fuck. This was such a mistake."

Tears started to stream out of my eyes.

He came into the room and threw himself down on a couch in there. He bowed his head and clutched both of his antlers.

We were both quiet.

Except, eventually, I started sobbing.

He looked up at me, then. He bounded off the couch and wrapped me up in his arms. "Shei?"

I buried my face against his chest and clung to him.

He ran one of his big, thick palms up and down my spine, making soft, soothing noises.

This just made me cry more.

The harder I cried, the closer he clutched me, and when I finally managed to quiet myself enough to pull away, I looked up at him, and his eyes were shining too.

I touched his face. "I'm messing everything up."

"Hey, no, don't… you don't have to do that."

"Why couldn't I have told you to stay? Why couldn't I have let you know about the baby?" I looked up at him. "If I'd told you I was pregnant, you wouldn't have left."

"No." He shook his head. "No. But we'd hate each other right now, because I would have felt trapped, and I would have blamed you."

"You think…?"

"Maybe not?" He shrugged. "It doesn't matter. We had this crazy thing, and now it's all…" He pulled back to look at my belly.

"I had this really dumb idea," I said.

He looked up to meet my gaze. "Huh?"

"About… us and about how to…" I shrugged. "Why does it have to be all or nothing, you know?"

He tilted his head back. "All or nothing?"

"Okay, well, that resistance outpost where I've been living and doing admin work? I don't really like it there either." It was this very old building that was constructed right into a cliff and almost none of the rooms even had windows, and I sometimes felt claustrophobic there. "To be honest, one of the things I always liked about working for the resistance was traveling and going new places?" I didn't even want to admit this out loud, because of course my resistance work was selfless, no matter what it was that Holston said about it, even if he made it out like I was doing it to make myself feel special. "And before I was pregnant, I did field work and I traveled. I'd get a new assignment somewhere, and then I'd be on my way there? But having a baby, it means I need to be settled, and I can't go out in the field, and…" I sighed really heavily. "I can do the admin stuff. I don't mind the tedium. It's fine."

"Okay," he said slowly. He was confused.

"Sorry. I got off topic a little bit there. I guess what I was sort of thinking was…" I let out a breath. "I could do a lot of that admin stuff anywhere. They could send me encrypted files. I could pore over transcripts or listen to recordings wherever? I don't need to be… there."

He let out a long, slow breath. "What are you saying?"

"A-and if I had someone, like a person who I could really trust, to take care of the baby, like after she was older. Like not within the first gecycle or anything, but when she was weaned if I decide to breastfeed or… or… well, I could go on field missions again." I ducked down my head.

He shifted on his hooves. "Are you saying that you want…? What *do* you want, shei?"

"Would you let me do that? Let me leave to go on a field mission and be the primary caretaker for our daughter? Let me go do dangerous things and leave you here and not be a mom for… I don't know, maybe fogemoons at a time?"

"'Let' you?"

I gave him a little smile. "Okay, well, you know what I mean."

"You going to move in with me, shei? Are you going to be *here* with *me?* That's what you're saying?" His voice cracked.

"But not all the time. I would sometimes go, and you would sometimes go. You'd go on long hunting trips, just you in the woods, and I would go on missions for the resistance, and we would each let the other person have that."

"Yes," he said. "That's, um, that's… pretty much the most perfect compromise I could *think* of. You're brilliant, shei."

"I-I didn't mean to invite myself to live with you."

"No, please, invite yourself anywhere. I want you here. I want that more than anything."

He caressed my face.

I tilted my head back.

Our lips met.

I felt it everywhere, a shivery joining of goodness that assured me that everything was going to be okay, finally, after all.

I pulled away. "This *is* a good idea, isn't it?"

"It's definitely a good idea," he said. "We all need to feel like we matter, and sometimes we need more than just one thing. Or one person. A relationship might not be enough, and a job might not be enough, and a child might not be enough, but you might need... need them all?"

"*You're* brilliant," I said.

He laughed softly.

"Maybe it's... selfish though?" I said.

"Nature is selfish, shei," he said. "Nature is need."

"I need you," I said.

His face came close, and he rubbed his nose against mine. His voice was breathy. "No, you don't."

"No, I don't," I whispered, and then I was kissing him again.

TWENTY-THREE

sienne

"Oh, stars, Cypra, she's beautiful," I said, sitting closer to look at the holoprojection of the baby half-donen, who was currently kicking her blanket off with tiny, tiny little hooves, squirming in her mother's arms.

"She really is, though," said Cypra, grinning down at the baby.

"Is that a huuq?" I gestured to the stringed instrument, which I could see propped up against the wall behind Cypra.

"Oh, yeah." She turned to look at it.

"You play?"

"Not me, Holston," she said. "He keeps writing these silly little songs for the baby."

"How cute!"

"Well, they're all like, 'I'm the cutest and prettiest girl in the universe,' so our daughter is going to grow up very arrogant."

I laughed. "Oh, but she is really cute and really pretty, so I completely see where he's coming from."

"He's a very proud papa," said Cypra, grinning.

"Of course he is." I grinned. Then my smile fell away. "Hey, um, I'm sorry I didn't… I know we haven't really been talking," I said, picking at a spot on my pants, averting my eyes.

"It's okay," she said. "I've been so busy."

"Yeah, I heard about your plan to still do field work," I said. "That sounds, um…"

"It works well for Holston and me," she said. "He and I, we both have really strong independent streaks, you know? And we each need a thing that is our own. He has his thing, and I have mine, and we're, um, we're going to try to have it all."

"Yeah," I said softly. "It sounds sort of perfect."

She shrugged. "It's… there are going to be trade-offs and sacrifices. If I want to do this, I have to leave my baby girl."

"Yeah, of course you're really attached to your baby."

"I am." She looked up at me. "I can't even explain how attached I am, how intensely I love her? But Sienne, I want to go *now*." She let out a helpless laugh. "What I wouldn't give for just a day off, a chance to not be a mom, a whole night with my body to myself?"

"See," I said, still picking at my pants, "this is why I keep putting it off."

"Caspe said…"

"Oh, stars, did he tell you I was jealous?" I fixed a glare at the holoprojection, but it was Caspe I was angry with, not Cypra. "I am *not* jealous. That's not what it's about. I make sure, extra sure, that I don't get pregnant. If I wanted to get pregnant, I could get pregnant."

"O-okay." She blinked at me, a little taken aback.

I sighed. "Sorry. Sorry, ignore me. I didn't mean to take that out on you." I groaned.

"You can talk to me about it."

"He just doesn't get it." I shook my head. "But never mind that. Tell me about you. Tell me about you and

Holston."

"Uh, he's great," she said. "Like I said, he's the proudest papa in the history of the galaxy. He's all about making sure that he takes good care of us, and he…" A big grin slid over her face. "I mean, I love him. He loves me. It's, um, it's… I'm lucky, I think."

I grinned back. "Yeah."

"And you and Caspe are lucky."

"So lucky," I said. "We have a connection like nothing else in the universe, really. That's why it's so annoying that he doesn't get it."

She just eyed me.

I groaned. "What?"

"So, Sienne, if you haven't been jealous, why haven't you contacted me until now?"

I ran a hand through my short hair, sighing. "I'm sorry about that."

She waited.

"Okay, maybe I am jealous," I said in a low voice, shaking my head. "But… but I think it's just that it happened accidentally. If I was accidentally pregnant, it would be fine. It would be something I had to deal with, and I would deal with it. But if I have to choose it…"

"I get that," she said, nodding. "But seriously, Sienne, if you're jealous of people accidentally getting pregnant, don't you think that means you want to be pregnant on purpose?"

"It's only that everyone I run into, in the entire galaxy, ends up married and pregnant and happy, right?"

"Everyone?" she said.

"Yes," I said. "It doesn't even make any sense. Like how could that be real? It's ridiculous. Not everyone gets a happily ever after."

She considered. "Maybe it depends on how you, um, look at it? Because if I told you that my baby was only two gemoons old and that her father had been out on overnight hunting trips—just one night—at least five times since she was born, and left me all alone, you might think that didn't sound entirely like happily ever after, and you might not believe that I liked it when he wasn't around sometimes, because... too much." She made a face.

I laughed. "No, I get that. Men, right? Needy."

"So needy," she said, shaking her head. "What is that?"

I shrugged. "I don't know. Some kind of compensation for the ability to open hatch door cranks one handed? Like, nature is like, 'We will make them physically stronger and, as a balance, deep down vulnerable.'"

"Maybe," she said, laughing. "Anyway, I'm just saying, it's *my* happily ever after. We all have the ability to tell ourselves our own stories. Sometimes, we have to give ourselves permission to want what we want without feeling ashamed of it." She shrugged.

"That's true," I said. I knew exactly what she meant. For a long time, I couldn't allow myself to admit that I wanted Caspe, because I felt like I shouldn't want him.

Was the baby thing similar at all?

Several hihors later, after I'd ended the communication with Cypra, and we'd made plans to meet up once she was back in the field, and I'd cooed over how cute her sweet little girl was, I found Caspe in his tank of water. He had to soak in it for a certain amount of time every day. Sometimes I joined him there.

Sometimes, he put his tentacles in all kinds of naughty places while I joined him.

But this time, I didn't want to be distracted, so I just leaned on the lip and peered in at him. "I made up with Cypra today. I saw her baby."

"Oh?" he said. "We doing this now, then?"

"Doing what now?"

"The showdown," he said. "Where our little argument about this stops being polite?"

I straightened. "You're angry with me?"

"*You're* angry with *me*."

"Caspe..." I let out an exasperated breath.

"See?" He rose up in the water, tentacles surfacing. "You want to get it on? You want to put a blaster on me? You want—"

"No, I don't want to do anything to you."

"So, you want me to restrain you with my tentacles and maybe spank you a—"

"Every fight we have does not have to turn into sex!"

He sank back down into the water, disappointed. "But doesn't it usually, though?"

I sighed, shaking my head. "Caspe, if we have a baby, who are we even going to *be?*"

He was quiet.

I looked up at him.

"You think it's going to change who we are, sweetheart?" he said in a low voice.

"Don't you?"

"I think it's kind of an adventure," he said. "We don't know what will happen. But I'm sure we can handle it."

I licked my lips. "What if... what if it never happens?"

He went still.

I eyed him.

He used his tentacles to pull himself up, dripping, out of the water. He came for me, but I backed away, shaking my head.

"Don't get me all wet."

He stopped.

"You know what?" I raised both of my hands. "Never mind."

"Hey, Sienne, you don't want to have babies at all?" His voice sounded odd, flattened in some strange way.

"I didn't say that!" I turned around.

"You can say that," he said, his voice still that weird flat sound, though. "If that's how you really feel, I want to know."

"*You* want babies," I said, turning back to face him.

"I want you more." This was immediate, stronger.

I hesitated.

"That can be okay." He was coming closer, and his voice was gentle now, and his tentacles were coming up around me, all around, reassuring caresses.

"I don't know." The truth was, when I thought about being a mother, I felt panicked, but when I thought about *never* being a mother, I felt panicked about that prospect too. "What if I said that now, and then at some point, I changed my mind?"

"Said that you didn't want children at all right now, you mean?"

"Yeah, but then, like five gecycles from now, I decided I do? W-would you...?"

"That would be, uh, I'm not saying that would be entirely the easiest adjustment to make," he said. "But to be honest, it wouldn't be that much different than things are now, which is that you keep saying, 'Not yet,' and I'm really okay with that."

"No, you're not."

"*Sienne,* it's obviously so much of a bigger deal for you than it is for me. You have to grow the baby in your *body*."

"Unless we wanted to adopt or something."

"Is that what you want?"

"I don't know."

He laughed, pulling me even closer, his tentacles wrapping me up and bringing me against his sleek, slippery chest.

I put both of my hands against his pectoral muscles. "Well, if you're okay with me being undecided about it all, why are we fighting about this?"

"I don't know."

I rolled my eyes. "You're not okay with it."

"I think you're not okay with it," he said. "I think you want it decided one way or the other."

I sighed.

"What if we, like, start flipping a coin about whether or not we use spermicide patches," he said. "Leave it up to fate."

I blinked. "But then I might get pregnant."

He nodded at me.

I dragged my hands down his chest. "Caspe..." I gasped. "Caspe, Caspe, Caspe."

His mouth found mine.

I clung to him.

www.ingramcontent.com/pod-product-compliance
Lightning Source LLC
LaVergne TN
LVHW091304150826
845673LV00006B/1528